Timberline Hound

According to Old Timothy, Teddy was "a soft, fat maverick" when he came to the Colorado mountains, a boy who "didn't know a single thing every boy's got a right to know." But Teddy takes to outdoor life in no time, and soon is hunting and fishing and riding over the mountains with Mark, Timothy's hound pup.

Fast-paced and exciting, TIMBERLINE HOUND is more than a story of a boy and his dog; it is also the story of Teddy's daily increasing maturity and strengthening character, until at the crisis of the book he proves himself a hero.

Timberline Hound

Martha Miller [pseud. Ivan]

Illustrated by Brinton Turkle

Alfred A. Knopf : New York

For Gus, without whom this book
would never have been written

L. C. catalog card number: 63-9177

This is a Borzoi Book, Published by Alfred A. Knopf, Inc.

First Edition

Timberline Hound

1

The whistle-stop depot was a log shed in the center of a wide cutback into the mountain. It was fronted by a narrow wooden platform which paralleled the tracks. Steep wooden steps led down to a small parking space. A single vehicle was parked there, a battered jeep. In the jeep sat a slender woman, with close-cropped curly brown hair, tanned skin, and a stubborn chin.

The high mournful wail of a locomotive whistle brought the woman out of the jeep. She stopped for a moment at the bottom of the wooden steps and listened while the echo of the whistle bounced from mountain to mountain, gradually died away. Then, squaring her shoulders, she began to climb the steps.

Old Number Seven came huffing and panting up the steep grade around the side of the mountain. The engineer gave two short toots of the whistle when he saw the woman waiting on the platform. The locomotive ground to a stop. The fireman waved. The engineer leaned out of the cab.

"Hi, Pat Young," he shouted over the hiss of steam. "You expecting any livestock today?"

"My eleven-year-old maverick nephew, Jack. Got him aboard?"

"Yup. Only paying customer we hauled up. How's the book-writing business, Pat? Making a pile of dough?"

"Why do you think I'm still teaching school?" she countered cheerfully, then waved and started back past the baggage car toward the single old passenger coach at the end.

Kneeling on the hard plush seat, his nose squashed flat against the window of the coach, the boy watched her coming down the platform. His heart was hammering. She looked like her picture back home, only older, and now she was wearing cowboy boots and jeans and a fringed buckskin jacket.

He stood up, pudgy, round-shouldered, awkward. He tried to button his jacket over his fat stomach, then gave it up. He swiped at his stubby brown hair with one hand. His mouth was dry. He licked his lips, hoping wildly she would not want to kiss him. Perhaps if he had his hands full—he began to grab up bags and boxes.

4

She was on the steps, was opening the coach door. "Hi, Teddy," she called cheerfully. "I'm your Aunt Patricia. Don't guess you remember me. After all, you weren't quite five when we last met. Welcome to Thunder River."

"H'lo," he muttered, dropping a bag, stooping to pick it up, then dropping a box.

"Here, let me help." His aunt retrieved the box, picked up a bag. "Got everything? Let's go."

The engineer gave them a piercing blast of the whistle, waved. Steam hissed. Wheels ground. The train pulled slowly away with deafening clatter.

"Down the steps here," Patricia shouted over the din. "Careful, they're narrow."

They stowed Teddy's luggage in the back of the jeep and climbed in. The boy cleared his throat nervously.

"Can we stop in town, Aunt Patricia? I want to buy me a *TV Guide.*"

She looked at him, a vertical line between her dark brows. "Teddy, I'm sorry, but there just isn't any town. Nearest thing is the Trading Post, and that's twenty miles over the mountains."

"Golly." The boy twisted around, stared at the towering, snow-crested mountains, the long green sweeps of spruce and pine and aspen, the sheer drop of granite cliffs to the racing, churning mountain river far below. "Colorado is sure different from back home," he said glumly.

She kicked the starter, gunned the motor, drove recklessly off down the rocky, twisting road. "I imagine you'll find it a lot different, Teddy, but I'm hoping you'll learn to love Thunder River Canyon. Lots of people save their money for years, just to have a vacation here."

The boy clung to the side of the jeep, shutting his eyes against the sickening blur of mountain and canyon as they skidded around a hairpin turn. He did not answer.

"Some people like to get away from TV and traffic and telephones," she went on, gunning the motor as she put the jeep to a steep grade.

Teddy's eyes flew open. He stared at his aunt openmouthed. "You mean you don't even have a TV?" he asked unbelievingly.

She shook her head. "Mountains interfere. No booster stations. Look, Teddy, up there in the timber on the right. Mule deer buck."

The boy half rose in his seat, stared at the buck. "How come his antlers are so little?"

"He shed his old ones in the spring. His new ones are just growing out."

"Oh." Teddy sat back and looked at his aunt. "What do you do out here," he asked, "without TV, I mean?"

"Ride horseback," she told him, "read, fish, hunt."

Teddy said nothing. He stared hard at the dashboard. He had never held a real gun in his hands. Horses. He shivered. He had been fishing once with his friend Clarence and Uncle Ed, and had sat all morning in a boat holding a cane pole. He had caught a fish at the very last, a little fish, but when he jerked it out, he had tangled his line in a tree at the water's edge. Clarence and Uncle Ed had laughed at him.

The road dipped suddenly down the side of the moun-

6

tain, crossed the churning, roaring stream on a low bridge, and climbed out onto a wide flat of towering pines and deep drifts of brown needles.

Without warning Patricia pulled off to one side of the road, cut the motor, twisted around on the seat to face her nephew. "You know, Teddy," she said gently, "it might be a good idea if you and I had a little conference."

He would not look at her. "Conference?" he echoed suspiciously.

"Well, talk, then. I know it's awfully hard for you to leave your friends, move to a strange place, live with an aunt you don't even know. And it's twice as hard so soon after your losing your father. I didn't know your father very well. In fact, I only met him twice—when my sister, your mother, and he got married, and then later on when your mother died."

"Yes'm, Dad told me," the boy muttered.

"And then when the telegram came about his dying, I was in the hospital with pneumonia. I would have come East for his funeral if I could have, Teddy."

The boy stared hard at the dashboard, lips tight. "That was all right," he said after a moment. "Uncle Ed and Aunt Helen—they're Clarence's parents—Clarence is my roommate at school—well, they were swell. They're really more like my folks than—than—"

"Than I am?" she asked quietly.

He reddened. "No'm, that is, I wasn't thinking about you. It was my dad. I never saw him much, not like the other fellows did their dads. His job kept him gone most of the time. That's why he fixed it so's I spent my vacations with Uncle Ed and Aunt Helen. They were his best friends, you know. I usually went home with Clarence weekends, too."

"You were a lucky boy to have such good friends," his aunt said warmly. "I had a long letter from Mrs. Burke after your father died. They sound like kind people."

"They're swell." He looked at her then, brown eyes lighting. "You ought to see their place. A swimming pool and a tennis court and a billiard table in the den and a real soda-fountain bar and—"

"A soda-fountain bar?"

"Yes'm. Aunt Helen loves ice cream. Keeps all kinds of flavors and chocolate sauce and nuts and stuff like that. I bet me and Clarence never ate two regular meals any weekend. We even ate sodas and sundaes for breakfast. Boy!"

Patricia's glance slid over her nephew's fat body. "Mmmm," she murmured. "Well, I'm afraid I don't have a soda-fountain bar at the cabin, but we'll manage, Teddy. Coming from New York to this high altitude is going to give you such an appetite that plain old food will taste good to you."

She started the motor, pulled back out onto the road. Mile after mile fell behind them. They were climbing steadily. The pines on the lower slopes had given way to big spruce and thick stands of aspen. Sunlight filtered down palely on slender white trunks.

As Patricia maneuvered the jeep between two giant boulders toppled beside the road, Teddy turned to her, face pale. "I think I'm going to be sick," he announced miserably.

"Oh, Teddy!" She stepped on the brake. "Sick at your stomach?"

"I don't know," he gasped. He took a deep breath. "Ever since the train left Denver, my heart's been pounding like crazy, and now my head hurts, and I can't breathe good."

"It's the altitude, Teddy. I didn't warn you, because I was hoping you wouldn't feel it. Some folks don't. You've been climbing ever since you left Denver. Right now we're almost nine thousand feet up. The change is too sudden for you."

"How long will I feel like this?" he gasped.

"A couple of days, maybe. The thing is, take it easy. Don't move around any more than you have to, right at first. And don't be surprised if you're sleepy most of the time, and hungry, too."

"You know, that's funny. I feel awful, but I feel hungry, too."

"Good for you. We're just a couple of miles from the cabin. We'll eat supper as soon as we get there."

2

The cabin sprawled long and steep-roofed in a clearing on the bank of the river. Built of unpeeled logs, it had a huge rock chimney and a wide unroofed porch extending out over the edge of the river on big cedar piles.

As the jeep rattled across the low wooden bridge, Teddy stared at the porch. "Looks sort of like the deck of a ship," he said aloud.

His aunt brought the jeep to a stop at the foot of broad wooden steps leading up to the porch. "That's about what it is," she said, grinning. "A lazy woman's fishing deck."

They gathered up Teddy's luggage. By the time they climbed the dozen steps to the porch, the boy was panting. He sat down on the edge of a redwood lounge chair. Above the pounding in his ears came the roar and crash of the current against boulders jutting up out of the river bed.

"Doesn't the noise bother you?" he panted.

"It's like music," his aunt said crisply. She had the front door open. Teddy followed her into a long living room with log-beamed ceiling and book-lined walls and a scattering of deep couches and bearskin rugs. Coals glowed in the wide fireplace across the room.

Teddy stopped stock-still just inside the door. He stared openmouthed at the head of a huge black bear mounted on the white rock chimney over the mantel. His startled gaze moved slowly down from beady black eyes over the gaping, grinning mouth snarled back over yellowed teeth to the long pink tongue. He swallowed. "Did you kill that bear?" he asked uneasily.

His aunt shook her head. "A friend of mine killed him. Fine old fellow by the name of Timothy Trich. Timothy was a famous hunter in his day. Stories about his hunting experiences still crop up in magazines from time to time. I've got a bunch of them somewhere."

Teddy said nothing.

"Timothy lives a couple of miles up north of here in Columbine Canyon," his aunt went on. "You'll be meeting him. I ride up every day or so for milk. Come along, I'll show you your room."

She opened a door to the left of the fireplace and led

the way out into a hall. "My room's there." She nodded to the right. "This middle door's the bath. Your room's here to the left. We'll dump your stuff and you can wash up while I see about supper."

When she was gone, Teddy drew a long tremulous breath and looked about him. The bedroom was long and narrow. The walls were logs. Through windows along one side the boy looked out at the chain of snow-capped peaks towering above a forest of evergreens. He glanced back at the room. At the far end was a double-decked wall bunk with red Indian blankets for spreads. There was a homemade desk against one wall, with book-filled shelves on either side. Beside the windows were a couple of canvas lounge chairs. On the floor by the bunk and between the canvas chairs were bearskin rugs.

There was a second door beside the hall door. Teddy opened it. Inside was a large closet with a rough wooden chest of drawers and a peeled-log clothes rod holding empty hangers. He closed the door. There would be plenty of time to unpack. He went out into the hall.

After he had washed his hands, he went back to the living room. His aunt had built up the fire and set a low table drawn up close before the crackling flames. Twilight was falling. Outside the circle of firelight, the room was dim. Teddy stumbled along the wall, fumbling along door facings for the light switch.

Suddenly a door at the end of the room opened and his aunt came in, carrying a large lamp.

"Hi," she said cheerfully. "Need some light?"

"I was just looking for the switch."

"There's one by the hall door and another by the front, but the current's off again. We had an electrical storm last night. They should have the lines repaired by to-morrow." She set the lamp down on the table and turned back toward the kitchen. "Sit down, Teddy. I'll bring the food."

He sat down slowly at the table. He stared fixedly at the bright flame in the lamp. He had never seen a kerosene lamp before, except on TV. Once at home the electricity had gone off in a storm. He and his dad had finally rummaged out some Christmas and birthday candles. Supper that night had been sort of a picnic. His dad had laughed a lot. Blindly the boy reached for his water glass, tried to drink down the lump in his throat.

"It gives a nice, soft light," he said determinedly as his aunt brought in a large tray of food.

"What—oh, the lamp." She put the tray on the table and sat down. "We have a big lamp hanging from the ceiling. Pulls down on a chain. Lights the whole room. I was just too lazy to bother with it tonight. Help yourself, Teddy."

Teddy eyed the tray. He took a thick slice of cold roast beef and two hot biscuits onto his plate.

"Fresh English peas straight from Timothy's early garden," his aunt told him, "and I just picked the water cress from the riverbank."

Teddy shook his head. "This'll do fine."

"Well, what vegetables do you like?" she asked.

"Not any, I guess," he said around a mouthful of meat and biscuit. "Aunt Helen always laughs and says me and Clarence sure don't go for rabbit food."

She opened her mouth, then shut it without speaking. They ate in silence. When they had finished she stacked the dishes on the tray and carried them out to the kitchen.

In a moment she was back with two generous slices of berry pie.

"I'll bet you and Clarence go for pie," she said tartly.

"Golly, yes. I've got an awful sweet tooth. Say, what kind of berries are these?"

"Gooseberries. They grow wild in ravines all over the mountains. Teddy, do you ever have any trouble with your teeth?"

His mouth was full of pie. He shook his head. "Not real trouble," he mumbled. "Say, gooseberries are good. I've got eleven fillings, but that's nothing like Clarence. I bet every tooth in his head's filled, some twice."

"You haven't touched your milk, Teddy."

"You got any chocolate milk?" he asked hopefully. "I don't like just plain milk."

"No."

"Sometimes I drink coffee," he told her.

She shook her head. "Not here, you don't. It's milk or water for you from now on, and I don't mean chocolate milk. Cow's milk, plain cow's milk, straight from Timothy's Anabel."

Teddy's headache turned bad after supper. His aunt gave him an aspirin and sent him to bed. It was cold in his room. He got into his pajamas, shivering. Back home it was already hot enough for air conditioning. Here the night was like winter.

Still shivering, he knelt down beside his open bag and felt through the layers of clothes until he found the photograph of his father in its silver frame. He set the photograph on the desk, turning it so that he could look at the smiling, handsome face from his bed. Then he dug a candy bar out of the suitcase and sat on the side of the bed eating.

The deep bearskin rug felt warm to his bare toes. He glanced uneasily at the window he had raised six inches. Outside the wind moaned around the cabin, rattling the window sash. From somewhere out in the darkness came the long-drawn-out howl of an animal. The boy shivered.

He finished the candy bar, blew out the lamp as his aunt had showed him, and dived into the lower bunk. He pulled the blanket up around his ears. Outside the animal howled again, high, thin, mournful. Teddy shut his eyes tightly. He longed wildly for the noisy, familiar dormitory back at boarding school. He longed for the easy laughing comfort of Clarence's big friendly home. He longed for his father. Two big tears squeezed out of tight-shut eyelids. He buried his face in the pillow and cried himself to sleep.

3

The noisy scolding of birds in the trees banking the cabin woke Teddy at sunrise. He stuck his nose out of the huddle of blankets, wrinkling it in the frosty air. Sunlight flooded the room. He squinted against the glare. From the front of the cabin came the muted roar of the little river. Teddy listened, yawning. Gingerly he felt his forehead. His headache was gone. He threw back the blanket and swung his legs to the floor.

Even that little movement set his heart to pounding.

He sat motionless on the side of the bunk until the pounding subsided, then got up, fished his sports shirt and jeans out of a suitcase, and put them on.

He could not button the shirt over his stomach. He sucked his stomach in, fumbled the buttons into their holes. When he let out his breath, two buttons popped off. A roll of naked fat bulged out through the gap. Teddy found a sleeveless sweater in the suitcase and pulled it on over the shirt, covering the bulge of fat.

He stuck his bare feet into loafers, hung his pajamas in the closet, then turned to his bunk. With precision learned from years in boarding school, he stripped the bunk and remade it with military neatness. Then he went out through the empty living room to the deck.

There was the spicy fragrance of evergreens in the cold air. Teddy took a deep breath. It was a good smell.

Slowly he went down the steps to the bank of the river. Grayed boulders, sides lichen-covered, jutted up from the edge of the stream. Teddy crawled out onto a flat boulder and stretched out on his stomach, chin overhanging the rock. Directly beneath his face lay a quiet green pool of backwash water in a nest of mossy boulders. Water cress grew thick along the edge.

The early sun beat down warmly on the boy's back. Under his body the boulder felt cold and damp. All at once he saw a flash of movement in the still water. A school of tiny speckled fish darted out into the center of the pool in tight wedge formation, hung motionless for a moment, fins quivering. Suddenly they wheeled with one movement, darted to the left, veered sharply right, and vanished through a narrow crevice.

The boy waited, scarcely breathing, but they did not

return. After a little while he rolled up one shirt sleeve and plunged his arm into the pool. He caught his breath at the sting of icy water. Leaning down from the boulder, Teddy stretched as far as he could. His groping fingers barely brushed the smooth white pebbles lining the floor of the pool. He drew back and rubbed his numbed arm vigorously on the seat of his jeans.

"Good morning. How's the headache?"

Teddy jumped. He scrambled clumsily to his feet. His aunt stood leaning out over the deck rail above him.

"Just about gone," he told her.

"Good. Want me to hand you down a fishing pole? A speckled trout'd fry crisp and tasty for breakfast."

Teddy felt a quick upsurge of excitement. He opened his mouth to say yes, then caught himself. In a clear flash he remembered that one little fish he'd caught back home, remembered the way Clarence and Uncle Ed had laughed when he tangled fish and line hopelessly in the branches of a tree. The sparkle died out of his eyes. He turned his head away from the friendliness in his aunt's face, scuffed awkwardly at a crack in the boulder with the toe of one loafer. "Naw," he muttered sullenly. "Fishin's for jerks."

He did not look up at his aunt. For a moment she said nothing, and when she did speak, the warmth had gone out of her voice.

"I'll put on the bacon then," she said quietly. "Breakfast in fifteen minutes."

They talked very little during the meal, but when they were finished and Teddy got up and voluntarily started clearing off the table, things got a bit easier.

When they carried the dishes out to the kitchen, the boy looked about curiously.

The room was long and narrow. Sink and cupboards were on the windowed side. There were no curtains to cut off the view of the mountain canyon with its thread of white river winding away as far as the eye could see.

While his aunt ran hot water into the sink and attacked the dishes, Teddy looked curiously from the gas range against one wall to the great black iron range which stood in the corner next to the living room.

"That's a wood-burner," his aunt said over her shoulder. "I cook with gas in the summer, but when winter sets in, I fire up the wood-burner. If you'll look down there on the walls on both sides, you'll see holes cut through for vents. A good roaring fire in old Betsy there will warm this room and yours and the living room."

Teddy took down a dish towel, still studying the wood range. He picked up a glass from the drainboard. "Golly, but old Betsy's a big stove, Aunt Patricia. Must take an awful lot of wood to keep her hot."

"Tons," she said cheerfully.

"Do you cut it?"

"Some. Mostly lopping branches off windfalls. Timothy cuts the stovewood proper when he cuts the logs for the fireplace."

"What's a windfall?"

"A wind-toppled tree."

"Oh. How come the wind blows trees down?"

"Well, some are old, and a good puff of wind will blow them out of the ground, roots and all. And then we have real storms up here in the mountains. That's when a lot of good sound trees get blown over."

"You said something last night about storms," the boy said uneasily. "Knocking down the electric lines and all. I'm not much on storms."

"Oh, you'll get used to them," she said cheerfully. "Mountain storms are exciting, even when they're destructive. Well, Teddy, as soon as you finish that plate, what say we go out to the corral and saddle up?"

He stopped his drying, gazed at her wide-eyed. "Saddle up?"

"The horses. It's my day to ride up to Timothy's for milk. You'll like Timothy. He's a character."

"You mean me ride a horse?" In spite of himself, Teddy's voice quavered. "Can't we go up in the jeep?"

"I wouldn't take even a jeep over the road up to Timothy's cabin. What's the matter? Haven't you ever ridden a horse?"

"Once," he said in a small voice. "In Central Park. I fell off and broke my arm. My dad was sure disgusted. I heard him tell the doctor so."

"That was just bad luck, Teddy. It could happen to anyone. Concho's your horse. You'll like him. He's very intelligent and he's sure-footed on mountain trails. Come along, I want you to see him."

The corral was at the end of a narrow trail which wound down around chokecherry and gooseberry bushes to the bottom of the slope back of the cabin. Teddy climbed up on the split-rail fence beside his aunt and stared apprehensively at the two horses that came trotting over to nuzzle her hand. They looked enormous to him and vicious, with black lips wrinkled back over yellowed teeth.

"This black beauty is Diablo," Patricia told her

nephew, slapping gently as the black bit playfully at her jacket sleeve. "Diablo's my pride and joy. I sent you a copy of *Wild Stallion of the Rim Rock* on your eighth birthday, remember? That was the first boy's book I wrote about Diablo."

"I think so," the boy said uncertainly.

"Didn't you read it?" his aunt exclaimed incredulously. "The book was dedicated to you."

"Well—" The boy's face reddened. He shifted uneasily on the rail. "I'm not much for this reading stuff," he muttered.

She looked at him for a long moment, her face a study. Then she turned back to the horses. "The buckskin is Concho," she said in a quiet voice that made Teddy squirm uncomfortably. "I bought him from Timothy when I knew you were coming to live with me. Concho's a top mountain horse. You'll soon make friends."

Teddy jumped down from his perch, jerking back from the inquisitive nose thrust at him through the rails. "I hope so," he said doubtfully, wishing he dared ask what a mountain horse was, but not wanting to, not after hurting her feelings about the book.

His aunt stepped to the ground and unfastened the gate. "Come along inside," she said over her shoulder. "The saddles are in the barn. Might as well show you how to saddle Concho right now. Then you can ride him even when I'm not around."

Teddy followed her across to the small log barn, managing to keep her between him and the horses frisking along beside them. Inside the barn his aunt took down a bridle from a peg and tossed it to Teddy. "I'll fetch out the saddle and blanket," she told him.

Teddy followed her outside, hopping so as not to step on the reins trailing from the bridle. His aunt dropped the saddle to the ground, slung the blanket on the fence, and seized Concho's long black mane.

"I'll hold him while you bridle him, Teddy. Get the bit in your left hand."

"This?" Teddy asked doubtfully.

"That's it. No, not like that. Your hand's got to be on the outside. That's right. Now hold it up against his mouth. Easy there, just hold it for a second. He'll open. There, now slip it in gently. Now take the headstall in your right hand. Ease it over his ear. Now the other ear. You're doing fine. Don't let him spook you with that head tossing. He's just playing. Now take that strap —that's the throatlatch—bring it under and buckle it. See now, that wasn't so bad, was it?"

"I don't guess so," the boy said doubtfully.

"See that post there—the one close to the barn door? That's a snubbing post. Grab the reins, Teddy, and lead Concho over to it. We'll tie him to the post, and then I'll teach you how to saddle him."

Fearfully Teddy led the buckskin over to the post.

"Concho's trained to ground-rein," his aunt told him. "Any time you want him to stand still when you get off, just drop the reins to the ground. But if you get off in timber, you must always tie him to a tree. Even a good mountain horse will spook in timber if a bear or a lion comes close, and we surely don't want you stranded maybe miles from home."

"A bear or a lion?" Teddy's voice cracked on the last word.

"There are lots of black bears in the mountains

around," Patricia told him. "They're not particularly dangerous, unless you scare them. Or go near their cubs. You avoid going close to a bear cub like you'd avoid a lighted stick of dynamite, young man."

"Yes'm," the boy stammered. "I'm not going near no bears. Did you say lions, Aunt Patricia?"

"Mountain lions, Teddy. They're not as big as the African lions you see in zoos, but they're bad medicine. Now, tie Concho to the post. That'll do fine. Fetch me the blanket and saddle."

Teddy lugged saddle and blanket over beside the horse.

"The altitude's really getting you," his aunt sympathized. "You're puffing. All right now, put the blanket on his back and smooth out all the wrinkles."

Eyeing the restive buckskin, Teddy lifted the blanket across the horse's back and smoothed it clumsily.

"Get it up over the withers," his aunt cautioned. "We don't want Concho turning up with a saddlesore."

"Withers?" Teddy echoed helplessly.

"Closer up behind his neck. The highest part of his back. That's good. Now, the saddle. Whoa, wait a minute. Always hook the right stirrup over the saddle horn before you throw the saddle on the horse. That way the stirrup won't flop down against his ribs and spook him. Up—up a little more. There, that's got it. Now squat down under him and grab the cinch."

"He'll step on me," Teddy protested.

"Nonsense, not if you look sharp. Go on. There, now you've got it. Pull it toward you. Through that ring there. This is the part you've really got to watch. The cinch's got to be tight, or else the saddle will slip under the horse and you'll really take a nasty spill. Pull it tighter. . . . That's still not good enough. Tell you what, Teddy, turn around and get the cinch over your shoulder. Now, pull. . . . You've got it. Here, let me show you how to fasten it. Well, you're ready to go. That wasn't so bad, now was it?"

"I sure couldn't do it by myself," Teddy panted.

"Nonsense, of course you could. Give me a minute to saddle Diablo, and we'll get going."

When she had saddled the black stallion, Patricia fetched a lidded bucket from the barn and hung it over the saddle horn. "All set?" she asked, coming over to where Teddy waited.

"Guess so," he muttered, scuffing the ground with the toe of one loafer.

"Come on then. I'll teach you how to mount."

He followed unwillingly over to the buckskin.

"Get hold of a fistful of mane with your left hand," his aunt directed. "Steady the stirrup with your right hand, while you get your toe in. That's it. Concho's too tall for you, but you'll grow up to him. Now grab the saddle horn with your right hand, and up you go."

Only Teddy did not go. Concho's ears flattened. He reared back against the reins with a loud whinny. He began to back in a circle around the post, with the terrified boy, clinging desperately to mane and saddle, hopping after him.

Patricia ducked under the reins and grabbed the buckskin's headstrap. "You hold still," she said sternly. "All right, Teddy, I've got him."

Teddy gritted his teeth. He swung his leg up. His foot slammed into Concho's flank. The buckskin reared with a frightened snort. Patricia pulled him down.

"Try again, Teddy," she encouraged him. "This time give a little spring with your right leg."

The boy tried again, failed, tried doggedly again and again. Sweat rolled down his fat face. When he failed for the fifth time, he freed his foot from the stirrup and backed away on shaking legs.

"I can't," he panted. "I just can't." He glared at his aunt, daring her to laugh at him.

If she were amused, she did not show it. "Come along outside," she said kindly. "We'll find you something to mount from."

She untied the buckskin and led him out the gate. Teddy followed, insides knotted with mortification. His aunt led the horse over beside a stump, held him steady while the boy clambered awkwardly up and into the saddle. Then she handed him the reins and went back for Diablo.

They rode up the trail past the cabin. Teddy gripped the saddle horn with both hands. His heart was pounding. His legs jerked and quivered against the saddle.

Concho sidled skittishly at the hollow clatter of his own hoofs on the wooden bridge, tossing his head till his black mane flew. Teddy shut his eyes, clenching his teeth against the wave of nausea that rolled up from his stomach. He opened his eyes as Concho swung left after the black stallion onto the road up the canyon. He glared at the buckskin's tossing head, glared at his aunt's erect back. "I hate horses," he muttered under his breath, "and I hate her, too."

4

The horses fell into a slow trot. Concho pulled up abreast of Diablo, Teddy bouncing in the saddle, his seat smacking leather.

"Bear down in your stirrups," Patricia told him. "It'll ease the jar."

Teddy obeyed. It was better. He relaxed a bit, let go his tight grip on the saddle horn.

"You'll be riding like an Indian by the end of the summer," his aunt said encouragingly. "This road goes on over to the Trading Post, Teddy. It's ten miles from the cabin. I'll take you over in the jeep one day soon. Nothing much to see but the Post and a little hospital and the schoolhouse where I teach."

"What do you teach, Aunt Patricia?"

"English."

The boy grimaced. "English! Me, I'm not much on grammar and that stuff."

"No?" she said placidly. "Anyway, I keep away from the Post during vacation, except when I need supplies. Tourists swarm the place in the summer."

"What do they do there?"

"Come to see the Indians, mostly. Most of the reservation moves in and camps at the Post during tourist season. They put on tribal dances for the tourists and sell pottery and jewelry. It's fun if you've never seen it."

"I guess." Teddy shifted gingerly in the saddle. "How much farther we got to ride?"

"About a mile. See that road there on your right? That's the Taylor place. Bert Taylor is the principal of the school at the Post. You'll like the Taylors. Elizabeth is your age. You and she should hit it off fine."

"Girls!" he snorted, staring at the two-story log cabin backed by tall pines.

"Elizabeth's quite a girl. Won the barrel races in the Rocky Mountain Rodeo the past three years. They're gone for the summer. Bert's doing graduate work in Wisconsin. That next cabin is the Tomlinsons' place. He teaches science, and she teaches first grade. They're in Europe this summer."

"Are we the only ones living out here?" the boy asked uneasily. "Except Timothy—what's his last name?"

"Trich. Oh, no, there are lots of summer people in

cabins hidden from the road. It just happens that most of my friends are away on vacation. The canyon buzzes during the winter. Square dances, ice skating, skiing, hunting. We turn to the right up there at the fork, Teddy. That's the road up Columbine Canyon, where Timothy lives."

They reached the fork and swung right up a timbered canyon. The road was two deep ruts following the twisting course of a noisy mountain stream. Willows and alders grew thick along its banks. The road climbed steeply between heavy stands of spruce and fir and pine.

The horses slowed to a plodding walk. Teddy looked about curiously. Timber almost blotted out the blue sky. Birds twittered from the trees. Long-tailed gray squirrels darted up and down the trunks. The ground was carpeted with brown needles. Bleached gray trunks of wind-toppled trees lay ghostly in the dim light.

"You mean this guy lives by himself way off up here?" Teddy asked, his voice sounding loud in the stillness.

"Timothy wouldn't live anywhere else," his aunt chuckled. "You dare say one word against his mountains, and Timothy'll swarm over you like a panther."

Teddy shook his head speechlessly.

"I suppose I really should prepare you for Timothy," his aunt mused aloud after a moment.

"What do you mean?"

"I'm not sure I know," she said slowly, "only most folks act surprised when they first see Timothy. He's not like other people. In the first place, he's got just one eye."

"You mean he was born with only one eye?"

"Of course not," she said impatiently. "He lost an eye in a fight with a grizzly years ago when he was young. He wears a black patch over the eye. It makes him look a bit fierce, what with his gray beard and the fact that Timothy seldom gets around to having his hair cut."

"Why was he fighting a grizzly?" Teddy asked, wide-eyed.

"He was a bounty hunter then. Sheepmen and cattlemen paid him cash bounties to kill off predatory animals. He'd been trailing a stock-killing grizzly with his dogs. The dogs bayed the grizzly, but Timothy made a bad shot. He wounded the bear, and the bear attacked him. Timothy got a shoulder chewed up and lost an eye before he finally managed to kill the grizzly with his bowie knife."

"Gosh! Is he still a bounty hunter?"

She shook her head. "He's a guide now, and a dog breeder. Guides elk and deer hunters during season; bear and lion hunters, too. He's built half a dozen hunt cabins up in the mountains around, so the hunters can take shelter if a big snow catches them."

"And he's got dogs!" the boy exclaimed, then caught himself, and added indifferently: "What kind?"

"Hounds. Registered hounds. Trains them himself for trail dogs. Timothy's hounds bring top prices. He was famous all over the country in his day as a hunter, and his dogs are trained right."

"I had a dog once," the boy said wistfully, "a wire-haired terrier pup. A friend of Dad's gave him to me. He was sure a smart pup. We named him Squeak, because that's about all he did at first."

"Squeak," she chuckled. "What happened to him?"

"Well," Teddy said slowly, "when school started, I couldn't take him with me. Dad tried boarding him in kennels, but Squeak wouldn't eat. We finally had to give him to a man in Dad's office who had a place out on Long Island. Dad and I went out to see him during Thanksgiving holidays." The boy paused, swallowed hard. "Squeak didn't even remember me," he said bleakly. "We never did go back. But Squeak was happy out there on Long Island."

Patricia glanced at the boy's face, biting at her lip. "Look, Teddy," she said brightly, "there's Timothy's cabin—across the stream and through the trees."

The cabin was small. It nestled in a clump of blue spruce in a grassy park which sloped down to the stream. Smoke drifted up from the white rock chimney. In front of the cabin was a hitching rail. Around at the back was a big pen, with a fence of vertical logs and beyond the pen, a log barn with split-rail corral.

"What are all those white things on the ground by the chimney?" the boy asked.

"Antlers. Deer mostly, and elk. Timothy picks them up where they've been shed in the timber and sells them to tourists down at the Post."

The horses splashed through the shallow, churning stream. From the pen back of the cabin sounded the loud barking of dogs. The cabin door was flung open. A man stepped outside. He lifted a hand in greeting.

"Halloo," he called out. "Come along. Coffee's on."

As they rode up, Teddy stared curiously. Timothy Trich was an old man, with a shock of gray hair and bushy gray beard. He was small, with a body as straight and slender as a boy's, save for a sagging right shoulder.

Timothy's buckskin jacket was worn, his jeans faded, his boots scuffed. The black patch over his left eye gave the bearded face a formidable look. The right eye, blue as the sky, stared fixedly at the boy.

They reined up beside him. Concho pranced friskily, head tossing. Timothy reached out, grabbed the buckskin's headstrap, held him steady.

"Well, Timothy," Patricia said cheerily, "this is Teddy Craig, my nephew."

Timothy said nothing, just looked. Teddy opened his mouth, closed it. His face grew hot. He wiggled uncomfortably. He glanced down, looked up.

"Well, lad," Timothy's voice boomed suddenly, "how do you like my Concho here?"

Teddy jumped. "Fine," he stammered, then broke off, flushing under the steady scrutiny of Timothy's blue eye. "That's not true, sir," the boy admitted miserably. "I'm scared to death of him."

Timothy nodded, looking pleased. "Can tell by the way you sit your saddle you've not ridden much."

"Not any," Teddy told him, face burning.

"Altitude must be getting you. You're puffing like a quarter horse that's run a mile."

"Yes, sir," the boy muttered.

"Well, time'll take care of that. How old are you? How tall? What do you weigh?"

"Eleven, sir. Four feet nine." Teddy paused. "Hundred ten," he added reluctantly when the old man waited, eyebrows raised.

Timothy tugged at his beard. "Some of that blubber's got to come off," he said at last. "But light and come in."

Patricia dismounted, waited while Teddy slid awkwardly out of the saddle.

"Just ground-rein Concho," she told him. "You passed your test with Timothy, bless you," she whispered as the old man turned toward the cabin. "If you'd lied about Concho, he'd have washed his hands of you. Timothy thinks a liar is an abomination in the eyes of the Lord. Come along."

Teddy followed her on wobbly legs. His pride still smarted under the old man's questions, yet there was a warm glow inside him. He did not know what abomination meant, but he had told Timothy the truth, and his aunt was proud of him.

The inside of Timothy's cabin was painfully neat. Teddy glanced about covertly. Drawn up before the fireplace were a couple of hand-hewn wooden chairs and a settee, all neatly upholstered with sleek, spotted skins. In one corner was a wood range with a row of iron pots and pans hanging from hooks above it, and a hand-hewn table, the top a planed-down slab rubbed to a soft grayed white.

In the opposite corner, a double-decked bunk was made up smoothly with turquoise Indian blankets. Covering the entire center of the floor was a huge bearskin, the dark fur tipped with silver. On racks along one wall were guns, their barrels gleaming in sunlight from a huge east window. Hunting magazines were piled high on a long table beneath the guns.

Timothy was busy at the stove with coffeepot and mugs.

"No coffee for Teddy," Patricia protested.

"Three-fourths milk, one-fourth coffee," he overruled calmly. "And two teaspoons"—he broke off, turned, the glance of his bright blue eye flicking over Teddy's fat body. "One teaspoon of sugar," he amended imperturbably.

They sat in front of the fireplace while they drank their coffee. The coffee-flavored milk did not taste good, but Teddy drank it down unprotestingly under the stare of Timothy's bright blue eye.

"Hear my dogs yapping out there in the pen?" the old man shot at him suddenly.

"Yes, sir. They're pretty loud yappers."

"Better be. Those are bearhounds and lionhounds, lad." Timothy chuckled. "Bearhounds and lionhounds've got to be loud. Know anything about hounds?"

"No, sir."

"Good. Won't have to unlearn you. Finished with your coffee, Pat? Come along then, I want to show my dogs to the lad."

They went outside to the pen. Timothy and Patricia were tall enough to look over the fence. Timothy pointed out a stump for Teddy to climb up on. The boy stared openmouthed down on a dozen dogs swarming with deafening roars up against the fence.

"Those big heavy reds with the long trailing ears are bloodhounds," Timothy shouted over the din. "The red and black there, that's a Red Bone. There's another. That one there's a Black and Tan. That's a Blue Tick there."

The boy nodded bewilderedly, unable to follow the old man's pointing finger in the seething pack of dogs.

"Well, what do you think of them?" Timothy bellowed.

"They sure look mean enough to kill a bear," Teddy shouted over the barking.

Timothy's laugh boomed. "Mean enough to try, I guarantee," he roared. "Maybe mean enough to do it."

"I hate to drink and run, Timothy," Patricia apologized. "But I've got to get back to work on the book."

"All right, all right," Timothy said and shrugged, turning toward the cabin. "We'll go pour up the milk."

Teddy lingered outside. He wandered around to the chimney side of the cabin and stood looking at the antlers which littered the ground. The dogs had left off their barking. The canyon was still.

An extra large set of antlers caught the boy's eye. He waded through the litter and squatted down, running his finger along the chalky tines. These would look good on the wall over his desk at school. There'd be no harm asking Timothy the price.

He got up and walked around the corner of the cabin. He was almost to the open door when he heard his aunt speak his name. He stopped, listening.

"—and I don't know how to tell him, Timothy," she was saying. "Of course, he hasn't mentioned going back East to school yet, but—"

"Just what kind of a fix did his father leave the lad in?" Timothy asked.

"There's enough for college," she replied, "and that just about covers it."

"Then he'll just have to go to the school at the Post," Timothy said with finality. "It's a good school. You ought to know. You teach there. Stop your worrying, Pat. You don't have the money to send the lad off to school."

"And do I know it," Patricia sighed. "The school at the Post is a good school, but there's that ten-mile bus trip twice a day and—"

"Doesn't hurt you, does it?" Timothy interrupted. "Won't hurt Teddy. You want the lad to grow up to be a sissy? Why, when I was a boy back in Massachusetts, I walked five miles to school and five miles home. Didn't know there was any other way. And we had snow every bit as deep as out here in Colorado."

"Yes, I know," Patricia said, half laughing, "but—"

Teddy turned, raced back around the cabin. He stopped when he was out of sight of the door and leaned against the warm chimney rock, his heart pounding. He felt sick. Not to go back to school—not to see Clarence and the fellows—his eyes blurred with tears.

There was a footfall beside him. Teddy whirled, swiping at his eyes with his fists. It was Concho.

"You!" the boy muttered, glaring at the horse.

The buckskin stretched out his neck, nibbled at the boy's sleeve with soft lips, nickered softly.

"Well," Teddy said in surprise. He stretched out a timid hand and stroked the soft nose, then gathered up the reins trailing on the ground and led Concho over beside the stump next to the pen. The dogs set up their clamor again, but the boy paid them no heed. Clumsily he climbed into the saddle, then swung the horse toward the cabin. At least Timothy would not get a chance to wisecrack about how he mounted.

They came out as he rode around to the door. His aunt flashed him a comprehending smile as she swung into the saddle, but said nothing. She reached for the pail of milk Timothy held up.

"Thanks for the coffee, Timothy."

"See you Friday, as usual?" the old man asked.

"I don't know," she said uncertainly. "Depends on how the work goes. I've simply got to get that book finished."

He nodded, tugging at his beard, then swung around and looked up at Teddy. "Well, lad—"

"Glad I met you, sir," the boy said politely.

"Yes, yes," the old man said absently. "I was just thinking—I know this aunt of yours. When she's working on a book, she ain't exactly what you'd call good company."

"No, sir," Teddy stammered, "I mean, yes, sir."

"Tell you what, lad," the old man went on. "Practice up on riding till you're good for a ten- or fifteen-mile run. When you're dead certain you can stick, you come, but not before. And I hit the saddle by six sharp, so don't be late. I can't abide tardiness." He raised a hand in farewell, turned back into the cabin.

All the way down the slope and across the stream Teddy puzzled over the old man's parting words.

"What did he mean, a ten-mile run?" he asked when he and his aunt were riding side by side down the rutted road. "What did he mean, me not being late?"

"Knowing Timothy, I'd say he was inviting you to trail ride with him and his dogs as soon as you think you're good enough."

"He's crazy," Teddy said incredulously.

His aunt shrugged. "You asked me," she said placidly.

"Well, I'm not going to do it," the boy muttered. "I'm scared of this horse and I'm sore all over and I don't like to ride anyway. I'm not going to do it."

They rode the rest of the way home without talking. They unsaddled the horses, then Teddy carried the pail of milk up to the cabin. His aunt poured it into jars and stowed them away in the refrigerator.

"Electricity's back on, thank goodness," she told the boy. "I'm going to work on the book now, Teddy. Why don't you unpack?"

Teddy put his things away neatly and stacked his bags in the corner of the closet. Then he sat down at his desk and wrote Clarence an unhappy letter, breaking the news that he would not be coming back to school.

At noon his aunt stopped work long enough to make ham sandwiches.

"How do you mail a letter out here?" Teddy asked as they sat eating.

"Our mailbox is up beside the road," she told him. "Just put your letter inside and pull up the little metal flag on the box. The mail carrier will pick up the letter when he comes by around four o'clock."

All that afternoon Teddy sprawled miserably on the glider on the deck. By sundown he was stiff and sore.

"Everyone gets sore after a first ride," his aunt consoled him at supper. "Take a good hot soaking tonight, then ride again tomorrow. That'll take out the kinks."

The hot soaking helped. Teddy went to bed afterward. The last thing he remembered was the faint peck, peck of the typewriter from the living room.

5

The moment he opened his eyes next morning, Teddy remembered. He would not be going back East to school in the fall. His aunt had told Timothy so. He squirmed down deeper under the cover, biting his lip hard, his eyes stinging.

When his aunt called him to breakfast he crawled out of the bunk reluctantly, groaning at the soreness in his muscles.

His aunt had set the table in the kitchen. She had made waffles and cooked little sausages. As they ate she chatted about yesterday's ride up to Timothy's, oblivious of Teddy's gloom.

As soon as they had finished doing the dishes, she turned to the door. "Ready?" she asked.

"For what?" Teddy asked apathetically.

"To saddle the horses."

"Have I got to?" he groaned. "I don't want to ride. I'm too sore."

"You've got to," she said briskly. She swung around looked him squarely in the eye. "See here, Teddy, you're out here in the West now. Everybody rides. Luckily, the folks we'll be seeing most are gone for the summer. You'll have time to learn. By fall, riding will be second nature to you."

That day set the pace. Every morning before Patricia settled down to work on the book, she and Teddy rode, sometimes on the highway, sometimes on an old lumber road up past the Taylors' cabin. They trotted and they loped and they galloped, with Teddy clinging grimly to the saddle horn, teeth clenched.

By the second week, Teddy was slapping the saddle on Concho with the assurance of experience. The soreness in the boy's muscles was disappearing. His face was pink with sunburn.

On Wednesday of the second week, Patricia sent Teddy riding alone. "You don't really need me anymore," she told him, "and I've got to get at the book. I'm way behind schedule."

Teddy rode slowly up the highway as far as the fork to Columbine Canyon. Impulsively he swung Concho up the rutted road toward Timothy's. As they rode in sight of the cabin, the dogs set up a loud barking from the pen. Teddy sent Concho across the stream and up the slope. The cabin door was shut. In the corral a Jersey cow lay under the shed, placidly chewing her cud. Timothy's horse was gone.

Teddy said nothing to his aunt about his ride. Next morning, however, he was up at dawn. "Guess I'll ride up to Timothy's," he said casually at breakfast. "Maybe I can catch him before he takes the dogs out."

"If you like," his aunt said serenely. "You might take the pail along and fetch home some milk."

Teddy held Concho to an easy lope up the highway. In the east the glow of the rising sun lighted the snow-capped peaks. Mist clung low over Thunder River. Above the rush and roar of water, the sharp clop of the buckskin's hoofs sounded hard and clear.

In Columbine Canyon, timber blotted out the sunrise. Teddy peered about uneasily in the gloom. He jumped when an owl who-o-o-ed from a pine.

They reached the ford. Concho splashed through the stream, broke into a canter up the slope toward the cabin. Smoke drifted up from the rock chimney. At the hitching rail stood a dun mare, bridled and saddled.

The dogs in the pen commenced to bark. The cabin door opened. Timothy stepped outside, cocked his eye at the sky.

"I was expecting you, lad. You're on time, right on the dot."

"How'd you know I was coming?" the boy asked as he slid to the ground.

"Saw Concho's tracks when I rode in yesterday. Knew you'd be back. Come in. Coffee's ready."

They sat at the table to drink. Teddy glanced into his mug, looked up in surprise. There was a twinkle in Timothy's eye.

"No need to report this to Pat," the old man chuckled. "Figure a fellow needs a cup of good strong coffee to start his day off right."

Teddy grinned. He had not smiled for so long, it felt funny. He relaxed, sighing contentedly.

"That day I rode up here with Aunt Patricia—I sure never thought I'd ever be riding up here by myself," he volunteered, watching Timothy.

"Figured not." Timothy nodded calmly.

"You did?" Teddy asked in surprise.

"Yup. Got to thinking, after you and Pat left that day. Maybe the lad's not cut out for the mountains, I thought to myself. He's a city lad. Maybe he won't ever cotton to the mountains. And even if he does, even if he learns to love the Rockies like me and Pat, it's still going to take time. A fellow's got to season to the mountains, just like green wood's got to season with the weather."

"I can ride pretty good now," the boy blurted, "but I still can't mount Concho, not unless I stand on something."

"And what's wrong with that?" Timothy inquired. "The buckskin's a mite tall for you at best. Besides," he added slyly, "you've got a right smart hulk to hoist."

Teddy flushed.

"Don't you worry, lad. You'll get the hang of pulling yourself up. Well, you aim to ride with me today?"

"I sure would like to, Mr. Trich."

Timothy picked up a battered old Stetson, counted the trout flies stuck in the brim, clapped the hat on his head. "Look, lad, you best call me Timothy. Been so long since anybody's called me Trich, it sort of gives me the jimmies. Timothy's more friendly-like."

"Yes, sir, Timothy. Where we going?"

"Going to run a couple of pups. They're the last of the litter and the best. Fellow from California is due here any day, a lion hunter. He'll take his pick of the two, and I want them both in top form. I aim to run them with Caesar every day from now on. Caesar's my strike dog. He sired both pups."

Teddy wanted to ask what a strike dog was, but he filed the question away unasked and followed Timothy outside. The dogs began to clamor when they heard them coming.

"Whole pack's crazy for a run," Timothy hollered over the din. "Wait here. I'll fetch out the dogs."

Caesar turned out to be a big, lank black hound, with rusty red chest and melancholy eyes between floppy ears. The first pup out was all-over black. The second was a half-grown replica of the big hound. The pups leaped excitedly up against Caesar, nipping, butting, barking. The hound ignored them. The red and black went galloping off around the cabin, nose to the ground. The black pup came tearing across to Teddy, crowding against the boy's legs, tail beating, pink tongue licking the boy's hand.

Teddy snatched his hand away and stepped back. The pup followed, head cocked to one side, sad brown eyes looking up beseechingly. Teddy glanced quickly at the gate, then stretched out a surreptitious hand. The pup licked it eagerly, whining, crowding up close.

When Timothy slid out the gate Teddy was gazing

off over the canyon, ignoring the pup crowded against his legs.

"Looks like you've got a new friend," Timothy said cheerfully as he barred the gate.

"Yeah," Teddy said indifferently. "What's his—what are the pups' names?"

"The red and black is Sheba. The one climbing your legs is Marcus Antonius. Mark Antony. Mark, for short. If you'll look at his collar, you'll see it there."

Teddy paid no attention to Mark as he followed Timothy around to the horses, but he was acutely conscious that the pup stuck close at his heels.

"Got to fetch my duffel," Timothy announced. "Won't take me a minute."

He disappeared into the cabin. Caesar flopped down beside the dun mare. Sheba was off down the slope, ranging along the bank of the stream. Mark sat down squarely on Teddy's feet, head cocked up at the boy, pink tongue lolling.

"Crazy fool dog," Teddy muttered, easing one hand closer to the pup. "Why don't you go down there with Sheba? I don't have no use for dogs."

Mark whined eagerly, licking the boy's hand. A delighted shiver went over Teddy. He snatched his hand away as Timothy came out of the cabin, arms filled with gear.

"Didn't you tell me before you ain't had much experience with dogs?" Timothy asked, sliding rifle and disjointed fly rod into saddle boots, slinging bulging saddlebags back of the dun mare's saddle. "Mark sure cottons to you."

"I had a pup once," Teddy told him. "A wire-haired

terrier. Only other dog I ever was around much was a poodle, name of Fifi. She belongs to my friend Clarence's mother. Aunt Helen keeps a ribbon on her topknot and her toenails painted gold. Sure sissy."

"Don't you be underrating poodles," Timothy cautioned, giving the saddlebags a final jerk. "They'd make the best retrievers, if only females'd stop pampering them. All right, lad, get your horse."

Teddy led Concho over beside a boulder and climbed into the saddle. Mark followed him, stood waiting at the buckskin's head.

Timothy swung into the saddle, gathered up the reins. "Now, lad, I don't know if the dogs will strike lion tracks, but if they do, they're going to take off like greased lightning, and the horses after them. So you hang on."

Teddy's heart quaked. "Yes, sir," he stammered.

"Well, then, let's go."

They forded the stream at the foot of the slope, then swung east up the bank, the dogs trailing. Teddy's mouth was dry. He licked his lips nervously, glancing back over his shoulder. The pup Mark was trotting easily beside Caesar and Sheba, head up, nose working. The boy glanced ahead at Timothy. The old man never looked back; he seemed to have forgotten the dogs completely.

The trail wound around through big spruce and pine, following the twisting course of the stream. There was the slap of current against boulders, the ring of hoofs on rock. All at once the brush cracked and a deer scampered away through the timber, then four more, white flags bouncing and floating.

44

Teddy looked back at the dogs. They seemed totally unconscious of the flight of the deer.

Slowly the trail began to steepen. They were deep into big timber. Pale shafts of sunlight touched the brown carpet of needles. All at once Caesar gave a short bark. Timothy reined up. Teddy pulled Concho to a stop and looked back. Caesar had left the trail and was snuffling over a low outcropping of rock to the right, the pups at his heels. Suddenly the big hound buried his nose in the brown needles, tail beating. The next moment he threw up his head, gulping in air. Then he was off, racing ahead through the timber, nose up. The pups streaked after him. All three vanished into the trees.

Timothy reined the dun mare over to the rocky outcropping. He leaned down from the saddle, scanning the ground. Suddenly he straightened up. "Lion scrape," he said quietly. "Get set for a ride, lad."

As if in echo to his words the dogs opened up from the timber ahead, their deep voices rolling back. The dun mare surged after them in a dead run. Concho lunged forward, almost unseating the boy. Teddy grabbed for the saddle horn and clung with both hands. His knees gripped the buckskin hard. Cold sweat soaked his body. He squinted against the tearing force of wind. Trees faded past in a sickening, grayed blur.

Then slowly the boy's body caught the rhythm of the running horse. He eased a trifle in the saddle, giving his body to the smooth rocking motion. His clothes were clammy with sweat. His heart was pounding. Exhilaration welled up from deep within him. He was riding!

Suddenly he saw Timothy throw up a warning hand,

rein the dun mare back on her haunches. Teddy pulled Concho to a sliding halt beside him.

"Shh," the old man said. "Listen. Can you hear them?"

The boy shook his head. All he could hear was the pound of his own heart, the heavy panting of the horses. Then suddenly the woods rang with a long-drawn-out bellow, then sharp, high, choppy notes.

"They see the lion," Timothy hollered, and gave the dun mare her head.

For over an hour the chase went on. The lion circled, cut over close under the south wall of the canyon, cut back into timber, down and up out of ravines, over windfalls, back and forth across the mountain stream.

The ride became a nightmare to Teddy. He made no attempt to control his horse, but clung grimly to the saddle horn and let Concho follow the dun mare. Sweat rolled down the boy's face. His forehead was scratched and blood-caked from the slap of a pine bough. His body ached. His legs jerked and twitched against the saddle.

All at once Timothy reined up on the brink of a deep ravine. Teddy pulled Concho to a stop, then slumped exhaustedly down across the horse's neck.

Timothy cocked his ear. "The hounds have faulted," he announced flatly. "The lion's given them the slip." He looked at Teddy. "You all right, lad?"

Teddy pushed up, chubby face pale. "I'm okay."

"That was a bit more of a chase than I'd reckoned on," Timothy told him, "but you did yourself proud, lad."

Teddy flushed. "I was scared to death," he admitted honestly. "I kept wishing I'd fall off and get it over."

"But you didn't, and that's what counts. Well, let's

find the dogs." Timothy touched the dun mare with his heels, sending her down along the lip of the ravine to the stream, then swinging east along the trail.

The trail began to descend sharply. Rocky outcroppings thinned the timber. The canyon narrowed. Far ahead the upjutting cliffs seemed to meet.

The trail curved close around a huge boulder. Now the barking of the dogs rang on the air. The horses picked their way along a narrow shelf of rock which hung out over the stream. As Concho eased around after the dun mare, Teddy caught his breath. Below lay a small lake, blue water rimmed by rocky cliffs.

"Sylvan Lake," Timothy called over his shoulder. "There are the dogs over on the south side. Up under the cliffs."

Teddy had spotted them. The dogs were milling along the base of a precipitous cliff. Their high, drawn-out voices bounced back weirdly from the rock.

"Aren't you going to call them in?" the boy asked.

"They'll give up and come in eventually," said Timothy, shrugging. "Let's find a likely spot to pitch camp."

The trail wound down a gentle grassy slope studded with clumps of blue spruce and outcroppings of boulders. Timothy reined up on the shore of the lake, close to the downstream riffle of the stream they were following.

"First thing is get a cooking fire going," he announced, swinging to the ground. "Then we'll see about catching trout for our dinner."

Teddy slid awkwardly out of the saddle. His legs felt wooden.

"Now, let's see," Timothy mused aloud, tugging at his beard. "Over there, I figure."

He led the way over to a rocky flat, ten feet above waterline. "No grass or needles to catch fire," he pointed out. "No peat to burn underground and flare up after we're gone. Here's where we'll build our fire."

6

While Teddy watched, Timothy chose three flat rocks and arranged them in a narrow U-shape. "Secret of a cooking fire is keep it small," he told the boy. "Trot over to that clump of pines, lad, and fetch an armload of cones and needles. And mind they're old and dry," he added as Teddy started off.

When the boy returned, Timothy's saddlebags were spread out across a flat boulder. A hand ax, a frying pan, two cups, and two plates were laid out neatly. A smoke-blackened coffeepot was balanced on the rocks of the fireplace. Timothy was just coming up from the lake with four freshly scrubbed potatoes.

"Put the stuff down by the fireplace," he said, "and pick up some good dry alder down by that clump at the mouth of the stream."

With his ax Timothy cut the alder into short, even lengths, then built a tepee of the sticks over a core of cones and needles. "Alder ain't the best firewood," he told the boy, "but dry, it burns good enough. And you don't have to worry about its exploding, like pine."

He struck a match, held it to the needles. There was a thin streamer of smoke as they smoldered, then a tongue of flame licked up over the cones. In a moment the fire was crackling. Carefully Timothy fed it with alder, moved the coffeepot back a bit, then sat down.

"Time it burns down, the coffee'll be done," he said.

Teddy sat down across from the fire. He glanced over his shoulder at the white cliffs. "The dogs stopped barking a long time ago," he observed casually.

Timothy adjusted his black eye patch with one callused hand. "They'll come loping in any time now," he said idly. He lowered his hand and looked at the boy. "That's the first thing you've had to say the past hour, lad. You don't talk much."

Teddy flushed. "Don't have much to say."

Timothy tugged at his grizzled beard, staring at him hard. "You're telling me when you've nothing to say, you don't say it," he stated flatly.

Teddy nodded.

"Shouldn't wonder but what you and I'll get along fine then," Timothy said slowly. "Ain't many, man or boy, can keep their mouths closed." He leaned back against a low boulder, easing into a comfortable position and pushing his Stetson to the back of his head.

"You know, lad, the wilderness here, it's a listening place. Chatter just doesn't suit. Look around you. The lake there, blue as the sky and quiet as a dove. Listen, you can hear the little slap of waves against the shore."

Teddy listened, nodding.

"And the white cliffs there, reaching up to the sky, and the mountains beyond—see the dark greens of the pine and spruce and fir and the pale streaks of aspen, all the way up to timber line—and then the snow on the peaks, glistening in the sunlight."

Teddy nodded, gazing about.

"The wilderness does things to a man," Timothy went on slowly, "good things. Out here with the sun sparkling on the lake and the sough of the wind through the big trees—a fellow can almost forget the mess the world's in, almost forget what cruel and senseless things man's doing to man all over the globe—" Timothy broke off, sat staring fixedly into the fire.

They sat on in silence until the alder burned down into a bed of glowing coals. Steam rose from the spout of the coffeepot. The air was heavy with its fragrance. Timothy leaned forward, poured two steaming cups, then carefully banked the coals with hot ashes, burying the potatoes.

"Time we've got our fish, the spuds'll be done to a turn," he told the boy. "Look, Teddy, here come the dogs."

The hounds came trotting down the slope in single file, Caesar in the lead. Teddy's heart quickened. Caesar went straight to Timothy, turned around three times, then curled up with a grunt by the old man's side.

Mark stopped ten feet up the slope, watching while Sheba went to Teddy and smelled the boy over, tail beating. Suddenly Mark gave a short bark and sprang down against Sheba, butting her away, shoving a cold, wet muzzle against the boy's cheek. Sheba moved off indifferently, went to curl up beside Caesar.

Teddy held his coffee cup out of reach of the pup. The boy's heart was hammering. He looked across at Timothy. The old man sat gazing at the coals, seemingly oblivious of the dogs. Teddy stared off self-consciously at the mountains. His free hand crept up and stroked the hound pup's side. With a tired whimper Mark draped himself across the boy's lap, tucked his muzzle against Teddy's stomach. He sighed. His eyes closed.

After a while Timothy stirred and got up, stretching lazily. "I'll fetch my fly rod," he told the boy, eyeing the pup in Teddy's lap slyly. "No, stay put, lad. No need to disturb your friend there."

He brought the rod back to the fire. Sitting down on a boulder, he fitted it together. "With all the gear old Maud's carrying," he said companionably, "we could camp out a week. Never have learned not to bring out more than's needed."

"Is that the mare's name—Maud?" Teddy asked.

"Yup. Heard a poem once, something about 'Come into the garden, Maud.' That mare's got a pesky habit of getting into any garden I ever planted, her and Anabel, my cow. That's how I came to name the mare Maud. I called Anabel after a woman I knew once."

He stood up, flicked the rod tentatively, then laid

it across the boulder. Taking off his Stetson, he selected a fly from the brim and carefully tied it to his line. "Not near as good as grasshoppers," he told the boy, "but till hoppers get plentiful, flies will have to do. Tie my flies myself. Bit of a camp robber's wing feather, a hair out of Maud's tail, hair off a mule deer buck—doesn't matter what. Don't go for those newfangled, store-bought flies."

Teddy nodded, trying to look knowing. Timothy went over to the saddlebags, pulled out a small net and battered old waders. He stuck the net in his belt, then sat down and pulled on the waders.

"Now we'll see about our trout," he told the boy.

With the hound pup at his heels, Teddy followed Timothy down to the stream fifty yards below its out-flow from the lake. Slowly they began to work their way back up the bank toward the lake.

Around an outjutting stack of boulders they came upon a deep, still pool. The old man waded out beside a log that lay in the water. Teddy squatted down on the bank, his arm around the pup. A trout was rising just beyond the tip of the log. Ripples circled until they hit the bank.

Timothy cast. The leader unfurled above the ripples. The trout broke water, slapped the fly with its tail, and disappeared.

Timothy reeled in, cast again. This time when the trout broke water, it arched above the fly. The old man struck. The fish was on. It dashed toward the bank, cut back across the pool, back and forth, tiring finally, moving in slow circles, closer, closer.

Timothy pulled the net from his belt, stooped, slid

the net into the water, and scooped up the trout. He waded out onto the bank, holding up the net for the boy to see the flopping fish.

Teddy caught his breath as sunlight touched the mottling of brown and green and crimson, the streak of scarlet along the belly.

"Gosh," he gasped, "it's big, isn't it?"

Timothy shook his head. "Under a pound and a half," he told him, "but sweeter eating to my notion than the big fellows in the lake." Carefully he lifted the trout from the net, strung it on a stringer, and lowered it gently into the shallow water at the edge of the pool.

"One more like that beauty and we'll have our dinner," he told the boy.

A trout was rising on the far side of the pool, the ripples circling wider and wider. Timothy waded slowly out into the water and began to cast, letting the fly float across the pool. Teddy's eyes widened. The fly looked as if it were alive. Its wings seemed to flutter. It beat its way frenziedly across the pool, bobbing with the ripples. The trout surfaced, came clear. The fly disappeared.

The fish fought, darting from side to side in the pool, water thrashing. Timothy played it carefully. It seemed to the watching boy that the old man knew beforehand just what the fish would do. Slowly the trout began to tire. It was swimming now in slow circles, nearer, nearer. Suddenly Timothy reached out with the net and brought it up.

The trout sizzled in the frying pan. Timothy crouched over them, eyeing them critically. "Once over, and they'll be done to a turn," he announced.

Teddy nodded, licking his lips. He was starved.

"Trot down to the bank of the stream," Timothy said over his shoulder. "Water cress grows thick there. Pull three or four bunches, and mind you swish them good in the current to get any muck out. They'll make our salad."

Teddy and Mark went down to the stream. The boy knelt down and pulled up great clumps of water cress. Carefully he washed the cress in the current, then sat back on his heels and shook the water out. He pulled a stem free and nibbled tentatively at the leaves.

"Not bad," he told the pup, running his tongue around his mouth, savoring the fresh, bitter tang. "For rabbit food, it's not bad at all."

Using the flat boulder for a table, they ate their lunch. The trout came out of the frying pan crisp and golden brown, the meat tender and flaky. The potatoes, skins charred by hot ashes, were mealy inside, the skins crunchy.

"Sure good," Teddy mumbled, his mouth full.

"Your water cress," Timothy reminded him, his bright blue eye boring into Teddy's eyes.

Obediently Teddy bit off a mouthful.

Timothy finished his meal and leaned back against the boulder with a contented sigh, nursing his coffee cup.

"A meal fit for an emperor," he said dreamily. "I recollect your Aunt Pat called it just that in one of her books. Slips my mind right now, which book. You happen to remember, lad?"

"I never was much for reading," the boy admitted embarrassedly, pushing back his empty plate. "I'd rather watch TV."

Timothy looked at him in amazement. "You mean you've not read your Aunt Pat's books?"

Teddy shook his head, not looking at him.

"I don't understand you, lad," the old man said slowly. "Pat's your own flesh and blood. I mean tourists make detours through these parts, just so they can get Pat to autograph copies of her books for their youngsters."

Teddy flushed. His chin set stubbornly.

Timothy pulled a battered old pipe from his pocket, filled the bowl from a little sack, tamped it with one forefinger. "Reckon this is the first time I've been a mite disappointed in you, lad," he said after a moment.

"There's lots of westerns on TV," Teddy said defensively.

"TV's fine," Timothy said deliberately, striking a match and puffing until his pipe drew. "TV's fine and good. But to my mind, lad, it ain't ever going to take the place of books. You take the out-of-doors, now. Nature feeds a man's body and his soul. But it's books that feed his mind, and his soul, too, for that matter. You show me a man who doesn't read, and you show me a man who's lacking. In a lifetime, a fellow doesn't get to know more'n half a dozen really smart people, but in books he can get to know the great minds of the whole world. Yes, sir, show me a fellow who's not a reader and I can tell straight off he's lacking."

Teddy squirmed. He shoved back from the fire. His face was hot. "Aunt Helen—she's Clarence's mother—she says reading gives her the headache," he said defensively.

"Stuff and nonsense," the old man snorted.

"Sometimes I get a headache when I study my lessons, Timothy."

"Now you're talking like a child," the old man said testily, his blue eye glaring.

Teddy looked at him, his chubby face innocent. "Well, I'm not very old," he said simply.

For a long moment the old man stared at the boy. Then slowly his face creased in a smile. Reaching across, he rumpled the boy's brown hair. "By golly, you ain't, at that. Keep reminding me of that, Teddy. You just keep reminding this old fool of that."

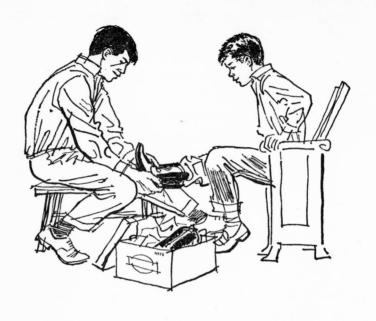

7

At supper that night, Teddy told his aunt all about his
day. She looked at him keenly when he said "Me and
Mark" for the dozenth time, but did not comment.
When he was finished, she merely remarked: "You and
Timothy seem to hit it off, Teddy. I'm glad."

"He's all right," he murmured, taking a big swallow
of the milk in his glass without seeming to notice what
he was drinking. "He's sure got some funny ideas,
though."

"Such as?" she asked dryly.

"I dunno. Like living in the mountains and looking at things and listening, stuff like that." The boy reached for a biscuit, then hesitated. "Are biscuits fattening, Aunt Pat?"

"Why, yes, they are," she answered, startled.

"Raw carrots?"

"No, not raw carrots."

She watched wide-eyed while he took a handful of the crisp carrot sticks and began to munch them.

"Me and Mark led the way back," the boy told her. "Timothy didn't think we could find the way, but we did. Guess Concho and Mark did most of it," he added honestly.

"Then what did you do?" she asked, hiding a smile.

"Helped Timothy feed the hounds. Went into the dog pen with him. That Mark—I sure thought he was going to eat Sheba up when she tried to get a hunk of meat away from him—then Timothy learned me how to milk Anabel—"

"Taught me," Patricia corrected automatically.

"Taught me," Teddy repeated, "and after that, I came home. Tomorrow Timothy's going to learn me—teach me, I mean—how to shoot a rifle."

Teddy took his bath as soon as they had finished the dishes. He called good night to his aunt at her typewriter in the living room, then went to his room. He squatted down before the bookshelves. Laboriously he read over the titles. At last he found what he wanted. From half a dozen books written by Pat Young, he pulled out *Wild Stallion of the Rim Rock* and carried it to his bunk. He switched on the reading light, pulled the covers up to his chin, and opened the book. The dedication read simply, *For Teddy*. The boy squirmed more comfortably against the pillows. He turned to the first chapter and began to read.

An hour passed, then another. The boy read on, lost in the excitement of the story of a boy hunter right there in Thunder River Canyon. The clock on the desk showed twelve thirty when he came to the end. The boy listened, fighting back a yawn. The cabin was still.

Pushing back the covers he got out of bed. Shivering in the cold, he went to his desk and rummaged out paper and pencil. He began to write, chewing on his tongue.

Dear Aunt Pat,
I just finished Wild Stallion of the Rim Rock. *It's the best book I've read in the last eleven years.*

> *Love,*
> *Teddy*

He got up and opened the door softly. His aunt's bedroom door was shut. Tiptoeing across the hall the boy slid the note under her door, then went back to his room, climbed into bed, switched off the light.

The weeks passed swiftly for Teddy. He saw little of his aunt. She was working feverishly on the new book, and he was away with Timothy from sunrise to sunset. At breakfast and at supper, however, he and Patricia visited. Since the night Teddy had slipped the note under her door, he had read the other five of Patricia's books. She was so pleased that she had let him read the manuscript of the new novel up as far as she had gone. Now, every night after supper she read aloud what she had written that day.

"Teddy makes a good sounding board," she told Timothy one afternoon when he rode home with Teddy for a little visit. "He tells me right off when my hero's not acting like a real boy."

"Teddy's not a bad sort," the old man conceded, grinning at the boy. "You tell your Aunt Pat how well you're doing with a rifle and a fly rod?"

Teddy squirmed uncomfortably, gave his jeans a hitch. "Naw," he muttered, his face red.

"Hearing that from Timothy makes me proud," his aunt said warmly.

Timothy fingered the black patch over his eye. "It's time we got the lad a fishing license and a gun permit, Pat. You think you might knock off work long enough to drive us over to the Post?"

"What about Thursday?" she asked. "That's the Fourth of July. Teddy'd enjoy the Indian dances."

"Fourth suits me fine. Well, lad, want to water Maud for me before I start home?"

"Sure, Timothy. Won't take me a minute."

When the boy was gone, the old man looked at Patricia. "I'm worried about the lad, Pat."

"About Teddy?" she asked in surprise. "Why?"

"Haven't you noticed the change in him?"

"Of course I have—a wonderful change—and we owe it all to you. When I remember how sullen Teddy was when he first came, suspicious of everybody and everything—why, he's not the same boy, Timothy."

"That he's not," the old man said soberly, "but you're wrong thanking me, Pat. You've got a hound pup to thank for the change."

"A hound pup?" she echoed.

"Mark," Timothy said grimly. "The lad's lost his heart to the pup."

"I know he talks a lot about Mark," she said uncertainly. "Are you sure, Timothy? About Teddy's caring so much?"

"Dead sure," he said flatly. "Dead sure the lad saves back the choice bits from his own lunch to feed to the pup when I'm not looking. Dead sure he talks baby talk to Mark when he thinks I'm not listening. Dead sure he hangs around the dog pen in the evening till I turn my back so he can hug the pup good-by, with Mark licking his face and whimpering because he knows the lad's going."

"Teddy's never had anything or anyone to love him before," Pat said slowly, "with his mother dead, and his dad too busy—"

"You know the funny thing, Pat; it was the pup that made up to Teddy at the start. The lad fought it at first. I got the feeling, somehow, he was afraid to love the pup."

"Of course he was afraid," she said hotly. "He lost the only pup he ever had."

"He told me," Timothy said bleakly. "And it's going to break the lad's heart when I sell Mark."

"You did tell Teddy, didn't you, that you've got the pup up for sale?" she demanded.

"Before he ever laid eyes on Mark, and every day since. I keep talking about Sam Wallace—he's the hunter coming from California—but I can't seem to make Sam come real to the lad."

"He'll come real enough when he gets here," she said

grimly. "I wish I could buy Mark for Teddy, but I can't afford to, not after buying Concho."

"If only Wallace will pick Sheba," Timothy said. "I can't stand seeing the lad hurt, but—"

"But you've got to sell a pup to tide you over the winter," she finished. "Oh, Timothy, what a mess, what a mess."

"Maud's watered," Teddy called, bounding in the door. "You know, Timothy, old Maud's a pretty good horse. Not anything like as good as Concho, of course, but—"

"But a pretty good horse," Timothy finished with a grin.

Teddy and Patricia were up before dawn on the morning of the Fourth. She had fried chicken the night before. While Teddy cooked breakfast, she made cheese sandwiches and sliced carrots into thin sticks, packed them in a big jar with ice cubes. As soon as they had eaten, they loaded the lunch into the jeep and started out.

Cars whizzed past them on the highway, all headed in the direction of the Post.

"Every tourist in this part of Colorado'll be at the Indian dances," Patricia grumbled.

Timothy stood waiting at the fork of the road. Teddy climbed over into the back and Timothy got in beside Pat.

"Thought for a while I wasn't going to make it," the old man grunted. "Was up half the night with a sick dog."

"It wasn't Mar—" Teddy caught himself. "Which dog was it?" he asked fearfully.

"Old Tiger," Timothy told him. "You know, the big brown-spotted hound. Must have caught himself a cold. Thought it was something worse at first."

Teddy let out his breath slowly. "The others—are they okay?"

"They're all right. That hound pup Mark—seemed like he knew I was going somewhere. Did his best to climb the gate after me."

Teddy sat back. He gazed intently at the rush of mountain side as the jeep sped along. A little smile quirked the corner of his mouth. Crazy fool pup.

The Post was a huge log building in a wide clearing. Beyond was a small rock building with the sign *Hospital*, and beyond the hospital, a large rock school building.

Cars were jammed bumper to bumper in front of the Post. Through the trees, Teddy glimpsed the bleached white tepees of the Indian village. His heart began to pound.

Patricia jockeyed the jeep through the timber and around the Indian village to the back of the Post. Teddy was hanging half out of the jeep. He stared wide-eyed at the Indians lounging in front of tepees, their pottery and jewelry spread out on bright blankets on the ground, and stared at the motley assortment of tourists in shorts and pedal pushers and jeans who crowded around the blankets.

Timothy twisted around. "Well, and what do you think of our Indians, lad?"

"Golly, Timothy! But why don't they all have long braids and blankets and stuff, like on TV?"

"Only the old ones still wear blankets and braids, lad. The younger ones—most of them are college graduates. The old men of the council complain, say the young men have forsaken the old ways—and I reckon they have, at least up to the point of wearing short hair and jeans and boots."

Patricia braked the jeep to a stop at the back door of the Post. "Boots," she muttered. "That reminds me."

They climbed out and went in the back door. The inside was a bewildering maze of tables piled high with merchandise, of narrow aisles seething with tourists pawing over pots, pans, blankets, piece goods, and souvenirs, of shelf-lined walls crammed with canned goods, guns, and ammunition.

One corner was squared off by post-office boxes and a stamp window. At a counter near by an old man punched imperturbably on a battered cash register, stuffed purchases into paper sacks, unruffled by the outstretched hands of clamoring customers crowding around him.

"It's not always this bad," Patricia said in Teddy's ear.

"Where did they all come from?" he asked bewilderedly.

"From cabins up in the mountains, and there are three or four dude ranches in the neighborhood. Let's see if we can get over to the shoe department. Coming, Timothy?"

"In a minute. You two trot along."

Patricia and Teddy worked their way through packed aisles to the single row of seats before stacks of shoe boxes. A young Indian glanced up from the moccasin he was fitting on an elderly man in Bermuda shorts and sports shirt.

"Hi, Pat. With you in a minute. Find a seat."

Patricia moved shoe boxes off a couple of chairs. They sat down. The customer departed wearing the moccasins, shoes in hand.

"Well, Pat," the young Indian said, "need shoes?"

"For my nephew here, Sam. Teddy, this is Sam Whitecalf, an old friend of mine. Sam, Teddy Craig."

Teddy shook hands in awe. "Pleased to meet you," he stammered. "Gosh!"

Sam grinned. He dragged over a stool, eased off Teddy's loafers. "Moccasins? Shoes?"

"Boots," Patricia told him. "Teddy spends all his time on horseback with Timothy. He needs cowboy boots."

Teddy looked at her wide-eyed. He said nothing while Sam measured his foot. When the Indian went across to the shelves, the boy whispered, "Aren't boots awfully expensive?"

Patricia squeezed his knee. "Not in the long run, Teddy. Besides, I think you've earned them."

Sam returned with an armload of boots. Teddy settled finally on a pair of dark brown leather trimmed with turquoise. He held his breath while Sam worked them onto his feet. Then he stood up, balancing awkwardly on the unaccustomed heels.

Pat knelt down, felt his feet. "Wiggle your toes."

Teddy wiggled obediently.

"Do they feel all right?" she asked uncertainly.

"I got them big enough to give him room to grow," Sam assured her.

"They feel swell," Teddy said, beaming, and craned his neck to gaze down admiringly.

"Well now," Timothy boomed, edging his way into the corner. "Well now."

In his hands Timothy held a brown leather belt with a handsome turquoise buckle. "Try this for size, lad."

Beaming, Teddy hoisted his loose flannel shirt. His aunt took one look at his middle. "Teddy! Your jeans! They're so loose they're down around your hips!"

Teddy glanced down crestfallen. He gave the jeans a hitch. "Every time we wash them, they stretch," he said apologetically.

His aunt got to her feet. "The jeans haven't stretched, Teddy. You've shrunk. Put the boots on my account, Sam. I want to take this young man back to the scales and weigh him."

At the rear of the store, Teddy climbed onto old platform scales. Timothy adjusted the black weights. "Hmmm," the old fellow murmured, moving the pointer over. "What'd you weigh when you first came out here, lad?"

"A hundred ten," Teddy told him.

"Hmmm. Hundred ten." Timothy peered at the pointer with his good eye. "Pat, you're starving your nephew. He tips in now at ninety-five. Good for you, lad," and he whacked Teddy on the seat.

"That's wonderful, Teddy." His aunt beamed. "Come on, this calls for new jeans to go with that handsome belt."

Teddy followed them through the crowded aisles, wobbling proudly in his high-heeled boots.

They spread their lunch on a blanket in the shade of a spruce. Teddy sat with legs stretched out flat, the better to admire the gleaming new boots. As he munched on a drumstick and raw carrots, he happily fingered the turquoise belt buckle pressing into his middle.

They were almost finished with lunch when the old man from the cash register came out the back door and spotted Timothy.

"Hey, Timothy," he called, "forgot to tell you that California fellow that was here last summer—Mr. Wallace—he called long-distance yesterday to reserve a cabin up at Kennedy's. Said he was coming to buy a dog off you. Be here Monday."

"Thanks, Henry," Timothy called. "That's Sam Wallace, the lion hunter I told you about," he told Pat and Teddy. "Glad we've whipped the pups in shape to show, Teddy. I'll be wanting you to help me run them for Sam."

Teddy looked at the half-eaten drumstick in his hand and placed it carefully on his plate. He swallowed loudly. "You figure he'll buy one of the pups for sure?" he asked.

"For sure," Timothy told him. "Sam's been waiting a year for this pup. Plans to build his whole pack of dogs around it."

Teddy's face lightened. "He'll want Sheba then," he said eagerly. "So's he can raise pups."

Timothy looked at the boy. One hand smoothed the black patch. "Could be, lad. Seems to me, though, Sam's already got a couple of female hounds. May be that he'll want Mark."

"Yeah." Teddy licked his lips nervously. "Maybe he'll

want that crazy fool pup." The boy pushed at the drumstick on his plate with one finger.

"Finish your lunch, Teddy," Patricia said firmly. "The Indian dances will be starting soon."

Obediently Teddy picked up the drumstick, took a bite, and chewed on it absently. "Guess I'm full up," he mumbled, putting down the drumstick and getting to his feet. "Think I'll walk around a little."

"Don't wander far. We'll want a good place to watch the dances," his aunt cautioned.

"No'm, I won't." The boy turned away, stopped, turned back. "How much you asking for the pups, Timothy?"

"Four hundred for the female. Five hundred for the male."

Teddy swallowed. "So much," he said almost inaudibly. He turned away, his shoulders sagging.

Timothy and Patricia watched the boy plod forlornly away through the trees.

"Sam Wallace has come real to the lad now," Timothy growled, tugging at his beard. "You see how he didn't say a word? Took his hurt away by himself, just like a real man."

"Drat that Henry for coming out to tell you Wallace was coming," Pat said miserably. "Why couldn't he have waited at least till we were ready to start home?"

8

Teddy woke up sneezing the next morning. His aunt
made him stay home from Timothy's. All morning the
boy moped around the cabin. At lunch he barely nibbled
at his food. Afterwards he took a long nap. When he
woke up, he put on his new jeans and boots and belt and
clumped out into the living room.

His aunt looked up from the typewriter. "Feel better?
Mailman left us something. Want to walk up to the box
and fetch it?"

The air was brisk and cool. The sun was warm on

his back. Teddy stopped a moment on the bridge, stared down at the rush of white water breaking around boulders. There were three magazines and a letter in the box. Teddy glanced at the envelope. His heart thudded. It was addressed to him in Clarence's big sprawling hand.

He stuck a finger under the flap and ripped it open. Clarence had written only a note.

Dear Fatso,

Things just ain't the same with you gone. Papa's taking me and Mama to Disneyland in August. Mama read your letter. Mama says I'm driving her crazy with you gone and nobody to fool around with. She says dont you worry. Your coming back to school if she has to pay your way.

Cheario Fatso!
Clarence

Teddy reread the letter. That crazy Clarence. Calling him Fatso, like always. Old Clarence's eyes sure would bug, seeing him skinny. Teddy sneezed, then grinned. He'd be going back to school after all, be seeing the fellows, be watching TV, be going home weekends with Clarence. No riding an old school bus for him.

Teddy gave the letter to his aunt to read.

"Fatso!" she sniffed as she began.

"All the fellows at school call me that," Teddy admittedly sheepishly, "on account of me being so fat and all."

His aunt looked up with a perplexed frown when she had finished the letter. "Exactly what did you write your friend Clarence about not coming back to school, Teddy?"

"Only that I couldn't come on account of there wasn't money enough," he said anxiously. "Did I do wrong, Aunt Pat?"

"How did you know there wasn't money enough?"

"You told Timothy so, that first day up at his cabin. The door was open. I heard you."

"But you didn't say anything to me about it."

"There wasn't anything to say." The boy looked at her bewilderedly. "You told Timothy Dad left just enough for me to go to college. You said you were too poor to send me to boarding school. Then Timothy said I could go to school at the Post. Remember?"

"I remember. Teddy, I'm not what you'd call poor. It's just that I don't have the boarding school kind of money. There's a difference."

"Yes'm," the boy murmured uncertainly.

She refolded Clarence's letter and tucked it back into its envelope. "It's very generous of Clarence's mother to say she'll pay your way, but it's impossible. She's a complete stranger."

"Not to me she isn't, Aunt Pat," the boy reminded her. "Aunt Helen and Uncle Ed are like family, sort of."

"Of course they are, Teddy," his aunt said contritely. "I keep forgetting." She got up, hugged the boy briefly. "You've just been here a month, but somehow already you're mine, mine and Timothy's." She handed Teddy the letter. "Anyway, we don't have to worry about this now, do we? Time enough when Mrs. Burke writes us."

"Yes'm." Teddy walked over to the window, stood staring up the road toward Timothy's. He felt funny.

Going back to school, being with Clarence and the fellows—but now he was family here, he and Aunt Pat and Timothy—she had just said so.

His aunt came over to the window. "Is going back to school the most important thing, Teddy? I've got to know."

The boy looked up at her. "I don't know," he said uncertainly. He glanced back at the road. No more riding up to Timothy's. No more helping with the hounds. No more milking Anabel. No more hearing the peck of the typewriter of nights from the living room. No more Mark.

He sneezed suddenly, a loud, explosive snort. His aunt burst out laughing. She handed him a handkerchief from her shirt pocket. He blew his nose hard. He began to laugh with her. She put her arm around his shoulders and they stood there at the window together, laughing like silly.

Teddy's cold was gone by Sunday afternoon. By sunrise Monday he was riding up the highway toward Timothy's.

As Concho swung onto the rutted road up Columbine Canyon he snorted suddenly, shied violently. Teddy grabbed for the saddle horn. He pulled the buckskin up. "What's the matter, boy? What's got into you now?"

Then he saw. Drawn up well off the road into the trees was a bright-red Thunderbird. Hitched onto the rear was a red horse-trailer. Car and trailer were empty.

Teddy reined Concho off the road and up to the car. California license plates. The boy glanced up the road toward Timothy's cabin. He licked his lips nervously. Sam Wallace must have already come.

Teddy held Concho to a plodding walk up the canyon. Before he came in sight of the cabin, he saw the spiral of smoke from the chimney. The boy began to sweat. Maybe Sam Wallace had already taken his pick of the pups. Maybe he and Timothy were sitting right now in front of the fireplace, drinking a cup of coffee over the deal. Maybe they'd have Sheba and Mark in the cabin. Maybe Mark would be sitting up close beside Sam Wallace, nose on Sam Wallace's knee.

A black horse was tethered to the hitching rail in front of the cabin. Timothy opened the door when the hounds started barking. "You're late, lad," he hollered.

Teddy dismounted before the cabin, ground-reining Concho.

"Come along in," Timothy told him. "We've got company. Where've you been the past two days?"

"I've had a cold," Teddy mumbled. "Aunt Pat wouldn't let me come."

Sam Wallace did not look like a lion hunter, Teddy decided privately, shaking hands with the tall, skinny, bespectacled man warming his backside before the fireplace. The boy glanced about covertly. The pups were not there.

"Timothy's been telling me about you," Sam Wallace said in a soft flat voice. "Says a month ago you couldn't mount a horse. Says now you mount from a running start."

"I've been practicing," Teddy replied, face red.

"Says you're getting to be a top hand with hounds," the visitor went on. "Killed your first lion yet?"

"No, sir," Teddy said, startled. "I haven't even seen a lion yet. Besides, I don't shoot so good."

"Teddy shoots better than he lets on," Timothy broke in, handing them steaming cups of coffee. "For a lad who'd never handled a rifle up to a month ago, he's doing right well. He can hit a tin can twenty feet in the air five times out of ten. Lad's got the feel for a moving target."

"Good." Sam Wallace nodded. "Now about the pups, Timothy. I'm eager to see them on lion tracks. From what you've been saying, I gather the female's better on unwinding a cold trail."

"That, Sheba is." Timothy nodded, fumbling with his eye patch.

"And the pup you call Mark—he sounds like the makings of a prime start dog."

"Mark's already a prime start dog. Beats Caesar nosing out a track just about every time. Right, Teddy?"

Teddy cleared his throat. "That's right," he said thickly. "Mark—Mark's a mighty good pup."

Sam Wallace drained his cup, held it out for a refill. "I'm a bit leery of a fast, quick getaway hound," he said slowly. "Prefer a slow starter that'll hold the line all day if need be. How do the pups tongue?"

"Not too much," Timothy told him, handing him his cup, "and not too loud. Don't worry about their holding the line, Sam. Both those pups can carry the line all day and still get downright enthusiastic when they tree the cat. Finish your coffee, and we'll go have a look at the pups."

Sheba and Mark came bounding out the gate when Timothy called them. Sheba went to Sam Wallace,

nosed over his feet and legs. Mark passed the stranger by with a sharp bark, made straight for Teddy, reared up against the boy, licking his face.

Teddy pulled back. "Down, boy. Down."

Mark dropped down, curling his body around the boy's legs, tail beating.

"Not hard to see who's been working the male," Sam Wallace said flatly. "Here, boy, here, Mark. Let's have a look at you."

Teddy pushed the pup toward him. Mark stood quietly while Sam Wallace felt him over.

"Both dogs have good legs," Wallace grunted. "Not too long, hind legs large enough, hocks straight. Let's have a look at your head, Mark. Hmm. Nostrils big and open. Sheba's muzzle's a shade longer, but Mark's is not so pointed. And both dogs have got good tails. Can't abide a hound that carries his tail dead level. Only thing I like less is a tail curving too high over the back."

He let the pup go, straightened up. "Going to be hard choosing between the two if they both run well, Timothy. When can we give them a try?"

"There's been a big lion prowling the canyon the past month or so, Sam. The pups have trailed him half a dozen times, but he's always given them the slip along toward evening. I figure they'd run him down if we stayed on his trail long enough. If you'd just as soon camp out, we can start out tomorrow morning."

"Good. I came prepared. Sleeping bag and gun are up at the cabin at Kennedy's. I'll fetch them down later. Can I leave my horse here tonight?"

"We'll turn him in with Maud and Anabel," said Timothy, nodding. "You best sleep here, too. That way, we can get an early start. Don't bother fetching anything else, Sam. Teddy and I'll get the rest of the duffel together."

Sam Wallace looked from the boy to the old man. "You're not figuring on taking Teddy tomorrow, are you?"

"Well—" Timothy began slowly, hesitated.

Teddy's heart lurched. He looked imploringly at his friend.

"I hate to disappoint the boy," Sam Wallace said flatly, "but I'd rather not have him along."

"If you're worried about the lad's keeping up—"

"It's not that. The pup Mark likes the boy too much. You know a good trail hound can't have two masters. If I buy Mark, and I've got an idea he'll be my pick, the sooner he forgets the boy, the better."

9

Teddy rode in home before sunset. His aunt took one look at his face and bit back her questions, busying herself with supper.

The boy barely touched his food. He answered Patricia's chatter in monosyllables. The desolation in his eyes took her appetite. She broke her rule and poured Teddy a cup of coffee when she poured her own.

"Tell me what happened," she said at last, while they sat drinking.

The boy looked at her. "Nothing much," he said bleakly. "Sam Wallace came."

"What's he like?"

"All right. He's good with dogs. He's sleeping at Timothy's tonight."

"I thought Henry said he'd reserved a cabin up at Kennedy's."

"He did. He's staying at Timothy's so's they can get an early start in the morning. They're going after that big lion me and Timothy tracked with the pups."

"But aren't you—" she bit off the question too late.

Teddy took a swallow of coffee. "Timothy was aiming to take me along," he said thickly, "but Sam Wallace said no. Sam Wallace thinks Mark pays me too much mind. Looks like Sam's partial to Mark." Teddy cleared his throat. "Looks like he's going to pick Mark," he finished huskily.

Teddy went to bed as soon as they had finished the dishes. He lay open-eyed in the dark, listening to the muted night sounds of the timber. In the spruce outside the window, a bird twittered sleepily. Wind soughed through the pines. From high on the mountain side came the melancholy, haunting wail he had heard that first night—the call of a timber wolf, he knew now. The boy's eyes burned. He thought of Clarence's letter tucked away in his desk. He wished it were already September and time to go away to school, time to go away from the mountains and the canyon. Tears came at last, and as he cried, he slept.

The day dawned bright and clear. Teddy awoke, stretched lazily. He moved to throw back the covers, then checked himself. He would not be riding up to Timothy's this morning. Timothy and Sam Wallace would be well up in the timber with the hounds by this time. The pups would be bouncy and eager. They hadn't been out for a run for five days now.

The boy pulled the covers back up under his chin and lay staring at the bright morning. Outside the open window, long tendrils of mist came snaking up off Thunder River, writhing and tossing as the wind caught them, slowly dissipating in the warmth of sunlight. A camp robber scolded noisily from the pines. From the kitchen came the sound of running water, the rattle of pots and pans.

Teddy got up and dressed, discarding the cowboy boots for his old loafers. Out in the kitchen his aunt greeted him briskly, but did not make conversation.

"I'll clean up," Teddy offered when they had eaten. She accepted without protest, and went into the living room to the typewriter. Teddy washed the dishes and put them away, then swept and mopped the floor.

"Think I'll go for a walk," he announced from the door when he had finished.

His aunt looked up. "Good. Which direction?"

"Oh, along the river." Teddy gestured down canyon. "I'll fetch back some water cress for a salad."

"Get a can of ripe olives from the cupboard and put it in the refrigerator then, will you? We'll toss the cress with olives."

Teddy found the olives, put them in the refrigerator, then went out the back door. The air was cool, and fragrant with the spicy tang of spruce and pine. The boy took a deep breath. Timothy and Sam Wallace had a perfect day for their hunt.

A narrow beaten trail wound in and around through the timber, following the twisting course of the river down canyon. Teddy walked slowly. A striped chipmunk darted out onto the trail, sat up on its haunches, head cocked, its bright eyes watching the boy. Teddy stopped. The chipmunk's nose wriggled furiously. Its whiskers quivered. Suddenly it was gone with a squeak and flurry of tail. Teddy walked on.

The timber was alive with the caroling of birds. As Teddy rounded a sharp curve, he came upon a deep translucent pool in a protecting half circle of upjutting boulders and jammed logs. A great spruce leaned out over the pool. The river had eaten away at the bank where it grew. A twisted tangle of roots gleamed white and ghostly in the quiet water. Teddy sat down beside the outleaning trunk, listening to the music of the river. From among the tangle of submerged roots he caught the swift shadow of a darting trout. He watched.

The water swirled sullenly between bleached, moss-covered logs which jammed the current. A pine cone came floating down, bobbing between boulders into the still pool, drifting slowly over against the twisted roots of the spruce, lodging there. Teddy leaned down and flicked the cone free, watched as it floated on down to lodge once more against the log jam at the lower end of the pool.

After a little while the boy got up and walked slowly down the winding trail. Except for the warbling of birds, the noisy churning of the river, and the occasional hum of an automobile from the highway beyond, the timber lay still. Ground squirrels and chipmunks darted among and over gray boulders scattered along the river bank. For a hundred yards a big gray camp robber flew from tree to tree along the trail, scolding noisily, darting down in sudden swoops over the boy's head. Then, suddenly as it had appeared, the jay flew away, leaving the boy to the crashing music of the river.

After a mile the boy turned back, climbing slowly up the canyon trail, searching the river's edge for water cress. A hundred yards below the cabin he found it and knelt down, gathering a large clump, swishing the muck from the roots in the river as Timothy had taught him. Once he stopped, holding his breath, straining to hear. There was nothing but the churning roar of current against boulders. The boy sighed. For a moment he had fancied he heard the faraway bugling of a hound's deep singing echoing down from high on the mountain side.

That night as he lay awake in his bunk, the boy thought he heard the singing of the hounds again. He got up and knelt shivering by the open window, but there was nothing but the sighing moan of wind through the pines.

Toward sunset next day there came the clatter of hoofs on the wooden bridge over Thunder River. Patricia got up from her typewriter and looked out.

"It's Timothy," she told Teddy, who lay sprawled on a couch with a book.

The boy jumped to his feet. His aunt had the door open. "Hi, Timothy," she called. "Get your lion?"

Teddy reached the door in time to see Timothy shake

his head. The boy followed his aunt out onto the deck.

"Come in and I'll make a pot of coffee," Patricia said hospitably. "Why didn't you bring your California friend along?"

Timothy dismounted. "Sam's gone," he said heavily, starting up the steps.

Teddy chewed on his lip, his eyes searching Timothy's face.

"Well, which pup did he buy?" Patricia demanded, cutting short the boy's agony.

"Sam bought Sheba," the old man said. He looked at Teddy, his good blue eye somber.

Before that look, the boy's quick upsurge of joy quelled. "Mark"—he faltered—"where's Mark?"

Timothy cleared his throat. "At the cabin, lad. Mark's hurt, bad hurt."

"Oh, Timothy!" Patricia protested.

Teddy did not move. He stared mutely at the old man, his face white, his brown eyes burning.

"The hounds treed the lion early this morning," Timothy said heavily. "Mark crowded him too close. Before Sam or I could shoot, the lion jumped. Got the pup with one swipe as he landed. Laid his right side open. I had a needle in my duffel, and sulfa powder. Soon as Mark had licked out the wound, I dusted him with sulfa and stitched him up with horsehairs out of Maud's tail."

"But you've always said never stitch up a hound's wounds," Patricia protested. "You said a hound will tear out the stitches—"

"I said never stitch a hound up unless the case is desperate," Timothy said simply.

Teddy stepped back involuntarily. He swallowed

hard. "How did you get Mark home?" he asked hoarsely.

"Carried him back in my arms, lad."

"What Aunt Pat said," the boy faltered, "I mean about him tearing out the stitches—"

"I put a muzzle on the pup before I left him," Timothy said reassuringly.

Teddy wheeled, started down the steps.

"Teddy, where are you going?" Patricia cried.

"To saddle Concho," the boy said bleakly.

"I'm coming with you," Patricia told Timothy.

He shook his head. "Let the lad come with me alone, Pat. He'll need you more if the pup dies."

The pale sickle of a new moon hung low over the mountains in the west when Timothy and the boy reined up before the dark cabin. The clamor of the hounds in the pen reverberated through the canyon.

"Best tether the horses," Timothy called over the din. "No use risking getting them spooked by some prowling varmint."

Teddy tied Concho to the hitching rail with shaking hands. His heart beat suffocatingly as he followed close onto Timothy's heels into the firelit cabin. Timothy switched on the light. Teddy choked back a sob. Mark lay stretched out limp and blood-soaked on a bearskin at one side of the fireplace. The boy ran to him, dropped down on his knees. With trembling hands he removed the wire guard covering Mark's muzzle.

The pup's nose twitched. He opened dulled eyes. His tail thumped. Weakly he licked the hand Teddy cupped under his muzzle.

Gently the boy stroked the pup's head. "His nose is so hot, Timothy."

"Fever," Timothy grunted. "I'm going to fetch fresh water from the stream. We'll clean him up and then keep his head sponged off. That'll help lay the fever if anything will." He took down a bucket from a shelf, lighted the lantern, went out the door.

Teddy crouched down close beside the pup. Mark stretched his muzzle over the boy's leg with a tired whimper. His eyes closed.

Softly Teddy stroked the pup's head. "You've just got to get well, Mark," he choked. "You've just got to get well."

Timothy found them like that when he returned with the water. He set the bucket down beside the pup. Taking off his jacket, he hung it over the back of a chair, then rolled up his sleeves. From a cupboard he fetched clean soft rags. Kneeling down he dipped a rag in the water and wrung it out. Gently he sponged away the caked blood and grime, careful to keep the rag well away from the wound. Four jagged, blood-crusted slashes ran from high up on Mark's shoulder all the way back to the hock.

"If we can just keep him alive till morning and there's no infection," Timothy said heavily, "he'll have a chance."

Teddy dipped a rag in water, wrung it out, and gently bathed the pup's face. "He's got to make it, Timothy," he choked. "Mark's just got to make it."

The night dragged on. Timothy made a big pot of coffee, poured two cups, then set the pot on the hearth.

"There's something I want to tell you, Teddy," he said gruffly. "Last night up there on the mountain, lying in my sleeping bag, looking up at the stars through the trees, I did a lot of thinking. The fire had burned down low. Sam was snoring away in his bag. Caesar and Sheba and Mark were curled up along my side."

Teddy listened without leaving off stroking the pup's head. Timothy paused, took a swallow of coffee, and wiped his bearded mouth with the back of his hand.

"I thought a lot about you, lad," he went on, "thought about what a soft, fat maverick you were when you came out to the mountains a month ago, thought about how you didn't know a single thing every boy's got a right to know."

"Go on," Teddy whispered as the old man paused.

"I thought about how fast you'd taken to the mountains," Timothy said musingly, "how you'd honed off your fat, riding and hiking and eating sensible grub. I thought about how you'd got over being afraid of horses, and I thought about how you'd come to love the pup here, even if you'd never once owned up to it."

Teddy hung his head. "I do love Mark," he admitted, choking up. "I guess I love Mark better than anything in the world."

"That's what I figured, lying there and looking up at the stars," Timothy nodded. "That's why I woke Sam up and told him."

Teddy raised his head. "Told Sam what?"

"Told him I wasn't selling Mark," Timothy said simply. "Told him Mark rightly belonged to you. I'd no right to sell the pup, I told him, not when Mark's given his heart to the lad."

"Oh, Timothy," Teddy choked.

"Sam took it pretty well," the old man went on. "After he'd gone back to sleep, I lay there studying. Me and the lad'll raise the pup together, I thought. We'll make a stud dog out of Mark. We'll be partners."

Teddy looked at him, his eyes shining through tears. "Oh, Timothy," he said again.

"If Mark pulls through, he'll be a long time mending," Timothy said heavily. "That hind leg'll be stiff for a while, but barring accident, we'll have him back trailing by the time school starts. What's the matter, lad? Why are you looking at me like that?"

"What you just said about school starting," Teddy stammered. "I don't know—I mean I never got a chance to tell you, with Sam Wallace here—"

"Tell me what?"

"About Clarence's letter," Teddy faltered.

"Who's Clarence? What letter?"

"You know, Timothy—Clarence—my roommate back at school."

"Oh. And what's this about a letter?"

"I showed it to Aunt Pat," Teddy said unhappily. "Clarence wrote and said his mama was going to pay my way, so I could come back East to school. I'd be gone—" his voice trailed off.

Timothy leaned over, poured himself a cup of coffee. He sat back, fumbling his eye patch in place with one hand. "Is that what you want, lad?" he asked gruffly.

"I don't know what I want," Teddy said miserably. "I do want to go back to school with Clarence and the fellows, but I want to stay here with Aunt Pat and you and Mark, too. What should I do, Timothy? You tell me."

"I can't tell you, lad," Timothy said slowly. "Nobody can. It's my belief that each person's got to decide for himself. Once a long time ago I tried doing what my father wanted. I went to college because he'd gone, and his father before him. After I graduated, I took a job in a bank, like he wanted me to." The old man paused, staring fixedly at the pup snuggled against Teddy. "Got so I dreaded seeing the sun come up of a morning," he added slowly.

"What did you do?" Teddy asked.

"One day I read something in a book—just a couple of lines, but they changed my whole life. I'll say them for you. I know them by heart. *If a man does not keep pace with his companions, perhaps it is because he hears a different drummer. Let him step to the music which he hears, however measured or far away.*"

"What does it mean?" Teddy asked uncertainly.

"Means people aren't alike. What makes one happy, won't make another. My father was happy in the bank. I was miserable. He was stepping to the music of his drummer. I wasn't."

"What did you do then?"

"Quit the bank, came West here to my mountains, found my happiness. My father never did understand. Mine was a distant drummer. I was the only one could hear his music."

Gently Teddy stroked the pup's head. "What you're saying is you can't tell me whether to stay here and go to school at the Post or go back to boarding school, isn't it?" he asked after a moment. "Because we're maybe marching to different drummers."

"Right. A grownup can tell a child, eat your spinach, don't fill up on sweets, wipe your nose, come in out of the rain, and he should tell—he's had more experience with such than the child has. But when it comes to saying to the child, you be a doctor or a lawyer or an engineer" —Timothy shook his head—"that's a horse of a different feather."

"Making up your mind is hard, Timothy."

"It is hard. I wish I could help you. I think I know what you should do, but then again maybe your drummer's too distant for me to hear. We'll know by and by. But you don't have to fret about what you should do tonight. Time enough later for that."

He got to his feet, picked up the bucket. "I'll fetch fresh water. The pup's fever'll likely be highest toward morning."

10

All that long night the old man and the boy crouched over the wounded pup. Mark's fever raged. Four times Timothy lighted the lantern and went down to the stream for cold water. Hour after hour Teddy sponged off Mark's hot muzzle. Toward morning Timothy poured water into a pan and held it under the pup's nose. Mark raised his head, lapped weakly.

"The pup's going to make it," Timothy told the boy gruffly. "He's past the crisis. Mark'll make it now."

Teddy let out his breath in a tremulous sigh. "I don't think I could have stood it, Timothy, if anything had happened to Mark. You think it'll be all right for me to get up a little? My legs are asleep."

Timothy nodded. He lifted the pup's head while the boy eased up from the bearskin. Mark opened dulled eyes.

"Stay quiet now," Teddy cautioned. "Don't you move. I'm just going to walk around the room."

The hound pup's eyes followed the boy wistfully as he tramped up and down the cabin. Only when Teddy came back, sat down with his back against the wall, and took the pup's head onto his knee again did Mark relax. He closed his eyes with a soft moan.

The sky in the east was paling to gray when Teddy dozed off. Timothy sat watching the boy for a moment, then got up stiffly and brought his sleeping bag and spread it out beside the boy and the pup. With gentle hands he eased the sleeping boy down onto the bag. Whimpering, the pup inched over and stretched out close against Teddy's side with a tired sigh.

Timothy stood gazing down at the boy and the pup. Slowly he shook his head. Then he fetched an old blanket and spread it over them. Wearily he went over to his bunk and stretched out.

The clamor of the hounds in the pen outside awoke them toward the middle of the morning. Teddy sat up, stretching and yawning. Anxiously he felt of the pup's muzzle. Mark licked his hand, tail thumping the floor.

"He's better, Timothy," Teddy cried. "Look, Mark's better. His nose isn't hot any more."

The old man rolled out of his bunk and came over.

Kneeling, he felt the pup's muzzle. "He's making out fine, lad. The worst's over, thank the good Lord."

Teddy laid his cheek against the pup's head. "Good boy, Mark," he crooned tenderly. "Good boy, Mark."

Timothy got to his feet. "Listen to those hounds. Bet your Aunt Pat's riding up the canyon."

Teddy got up, ran to the door, flung it open. "It's Aunt Pat, all right. Just fording the stream." He started down the slope at a run. "Aunt Pat!" he shouted. "Mark's going to make it! Mark's going to get well!"

"I couldn't wait any longer," Patricia told them five minutes later as she knelt stroking the wounded pup's head. "I didn't sleep a wink all night, worrying."

"Long as you're here, you can cook us some breakfast," said Timothy, grinning. "The lad and I were so busy working with the pup last night, we never once thought of supper."

Patricia got to her feet. "What shall I cook?"

"Flapjacks," Teddy and Timothy said simultaneously. "And a big thick slice of ham to go with them," Timothy added. "I'll go out and milk while you're cooking."

For five days and five nights Teddy remained at Timothy's cabin. On the sixth day he went home, taking Mark with him.

"It's the middle of July, and I haven't even been up to start repairs on my hunt cabins," Timothy told Patricia when she raised her eyebrows at the boy's bringing the pup home. "If I'm going to be ready for my hunters by elk season, I've got to stir my stumps. I've already signed up ten parties, and that's going to keep me busy. Besides, I want the boy to take over working the pup." He smiled wryly. "It'll do him good."

Patricia made Mark a soft bed by the kitchen stove. The first night she left the back door open. "So Mark can go out when he wants," she explained to Teddy.

Toward midnight she awoke, put on slippers and robe, and went out to the kitchen to check. The door was closed. Mark was gone.

Patricia ran back across the living room, out into the hall, and threw open Teddy's door. She switched on the light. "Mark's go—" she began, then stifled her cry. Teddy lay sleeping on his back, mouth open, one arm across the hound pup curled up on the blanket against his side. The pup raised his head, grinning at Patricia, tail thumping.

Patricia turned off the light, closed the door softly, went back to her room. Smiling, she took off her robe and crawled into bed.

A week passed. The angry red slashes left by the lion's claws scabbed over, peeled, were pale parallels of pink the length of the hound pup's black side. Mark's leg was stiff. Each day Teddy took the pup for a walk down the trail along Thunder River, going a little farther each time before they turned back.

Having Mark along on the walks opened up a new world to the boy. There was the day the pup led him aside from the trail into a trampled-down thicket of alders to where a spotted mule deer fawn lay motionless on its belly, with its long, slender neck stretched out flat, nose on the ground and big ears laid back. Only the large bright eyes, fearfully watching the boy and the dog, were alive. Sunlight through the timber dappled the thicket with splotches of highlights and shadows. Against these the spotted coat of the fawn made it almost invisible. Teddy would have passed the fawn by without Mark there to show him.

Timothy had told the boy how a doe would make her baby lie down and play dead when danger was near and she was forced to run away. Slowly he backed out of the thicket, the pup following. Now the doe would come back to her baby, would see they had not harmed it.

The only thing that ever got the hound pup riled on their walks was the marmots. They would sit on the slope up from the trail and whistle shrilly when the boy and the dog came in sight. Mark would stop and stand stiff-legged, head cocked, trying to locate the direction from which the whistle had come. Teddy could not help laughing each time it happened. He never told Timothy how a marmot would make the hound pup forget he was a lion dog, send him barking up the slope only to be brought up short in angry frustration as the marmot slid easily into the protection of a burrow under a boulder.

Two weeks after he brought Mark home, Teddy saddled Concho, and taking the pup, rode up to Timothy's. He held the buckskin to a walk the whole way. The pup's leg was still stiff. He kept up well, but he tired easily.

Timothy was sharpening an ax at a whetstone in front of the cabin. He laid the ax aside and felt the pup over critically. "He's coming along fine, lad," he said after a bit. "Let's see now, it's been three weeks since he got hurt. Time to take Mark up on the mountains and start limbering that leg."

"When can we, Timothy?" the boy asked eagerly.

"You'll have to do it on your own, lad," the old man said regretfully. "A blasted bear's just about wrecked my hunt cabin up on Lobo Mountain. I've still got a week's hard work to do on the cabin to get it ready for hunting season."

"Couldn't Mark and I go along with you up to the cabin, Timothy? I could help you work on it."

"That came to my mind first, lad, but the cabin's too far for the pup right now, and the trail's too rough."

"It's only I don't know if I can manage Mark by myself in the mountains," the boy said nervously.

"You can do it, Teddy."

"But what if he started a mountain lion? I've never even seen a lion yet."

"Chances are you won't see one this time, lad. The pup's too stiff to run a lion. But he needs to get on a trail, needs to get the feel of the mountains in his legs."

"Well, I'll try," Teddy promised. "I'll take Mark out tomorrow morning."

"And you take Pat's thirty-thirty along," Timothy told him. "With a crippled pup on a trail, you might have need of a gun."

Teddy's eyes moved slowly along the snow-capped peaks that rimmed Columbine Canyon. "Maybe I'll take Mark just a little way up Lobo Mountain, Timothy. Which one is it?"

"All right, look now. That peak at the dead end of the canyon is Bull Elk. That's where Sylvan Lake is.

The peak a little to the south is Lobo, and that taller peak behind Lobo to the east is Arrowhead. Spot them?"

Teddy nodded. "Lobo Mountain," he murmured. "I know a lobo's a wolf, Timothy. Aunt Pat says there're not many left around here. I still get the shivers when I hear one howl at night. Sounds so lonesome, somehow."

"May sound lonesome," Timothy said grimly, "but likely he's calling to his mate that he's just spotted a nice fat doe for their supper. I'll be glad if the day ever comes when the timber's cleaned out of wolves. If you do ride up on Lobo, Teddy, you keep your eyes peeled for them, and for bears, too. Bears are mighty touchy this time of the year, with their cubs still little."

"I sure will be careful," the boy promised.

Timothy walked over and sat down on the cabin step. He took out pipe and pouch, dribbled tobacco into the bowl, and tamped it tight with a blunt forefinger. "Been kind of lonesome around here the last couple of weeks, lad. Had half a dozen parties drop by, inquiring about hunting trips in the fall. Wasn't the same, though. Seems like I've already got used to having you around."

Teddy flushed with pleasure. He went over and sat down beside the old man. The hound pup followed, flopped down across the boy's feet.

"I've been lonesome, too, Timothy," Teddy said earnestly. "I sure will be glad when you're through working on the cabins, so's we can take the dogs out together again."

Timothy scratched a match with his thumbnail, held the sputtering flame to the bowl of his pipe. He sucked noisily until he had the pipe drawing. "Heard from your friend Clarence again?" he asked offhandedly.

Teddy shook his head. He reached down for Mark, drew the pup up close.

"Be the first of August in a couple of days," the old man said reflectively. He gave the boy a sharp glance. "You ought to be hearing pretty soon."

"I guess so," Teddy said reluctantly, arm hugging the hound pup close. "I guess Aunt Helen'll be writing to Aunt Pat pretty soon."

11

Patricia did her best to dissuade Teddy from going out alone with the hound pup next morning.

"Timothy must be out of his mind, telling an eleven-year-old boy to ride up into the mountains alone," she said vehemently, while Teddy was making a couple of generous roast-beef sandwiches at the kitchen table. "You don't even know your way around, except up Columbine Canyon. You could get lost. You could have an accident. You could die all alone up there before we found you."

"Aw, Aunt Pat," Teddy muttered uncomfortably, "nothing's going to happen to me. I'll have Mark along. Mark can always find the way home. Besides, Timothy told me to take the thirty-thirty along, just in case."

"Just in case of what?" she demanded. "Just in case you get tangled up with a mountain lion the way he and Sam Wallace and Mark did? Or a bear? What are you going to do if you ride onto a bear?"

"I'm going to get out of there quick," the boy said reasonably, "like Timothy told me to. Don't you worry about me. I'll be all right. You know Timothy wouldn't tell me to take Mark up on the mountains if he didn't think it was safe. Besides," the boy finished earnestly, "you don't want me growing up to be a dude."

That brought a reluctant quirk to the corner of her mouth. Smiling, she gave him a quick hug. "No, bless you, no dude in this family. Which way are you planning to ride, Teddy?"

"I told Timothy up on Lobo. That's where he's working on the hunt cabin, though me and Mark won't go that high. Timothy said it'd be too much of a climb for Mark so soon after getting hurt."

The morning was crisp and fine. Fleecy white clouds scudded across a blue sky. Teddy whistled a little as Concho swung off the highway onto the rutted road up Columbine Canyon. A lot had happened since that first morning he had ridden up this road with his aunt. Now the shadowy timber was neither gloomy nor scary. Now Concho seemed to know exactly what he wanted even before he was quite certain himself. He glanced down at the hound pup trotting ahead of the horse. Now he had Mark.

At the ford Concho pulled to the left, wanting to cross, but Teddy held him straight along the trail up the south bank of the stream opposite Timothy's cabin. The dogs in the pen heard the clop of hoofs on rock. They began to bark. Mark's head swung toward the cabin, swung back. Teddy grinned. He wished Timothy weren't already up on Lobo Mountain. Timothy would have laughed to see the pup ignore the barking dogs.

They began to climb. The trail wound through spruce and pine, up over a steep ridge, out across a grassy park. Teddy knew every turn. He had ridden this way with Timothy a dozen times since that first day they had trailed the lion up to Sylvan Lake.

A mile beyond Timothy's cabin, the trail forked. Teddy reined up. The left fork led on to Sylvan Lake, nestled high up on the south slope of Bull Elk Mountain. He swung the buckskin up the right fork. According to the way Timothy had pointed the day before, this should take him onto Lobo Mountain.

The trail climbed steeply. Slowly the pine and spruce gave way to thick stands of aspen. Wind rustled softly through the quaking leaves. Sunlight dappled the duff between their slender white trunks.

The steep climb was beginning to wind the buckskin. His breath whistled through his nostrils. Sweat streaked his withers. Just below a flat bench at the edge of a strip of blue spruce, Teddy reined up to breathe the horse. He glanced down at Mark. The hound pup stood with head up. He was sniffing the air as if he smelled something up on the mountain.

Teddy's skin prickled. Turning, he scanned the edge of the bench land above. He could see no movement in the clumps of spruce which dotted the rim. But there was something up on the bench. With his nose high in the air, Mark had started slowly up the steep slope. The pup stopped every few feet, sniffing uncertainly.

Teddy's heart was hammering. He slid the .30-30 out of its boot and checked it carefully. Then he put Concho to the slope, riding slowly on a zigzag course, so as to spare the buckskin. They topped out into a grassy park scattered over with clumps of spruce. The hound pup had stopped, nose up, tail taut. Teddy reined up beside him, staring.

Not a hundred feet away stood a large elk cow, ears pricked forward, dark neck-hair bristling. Teddy dismounted and knelt down beside the pup, one arm holding Mark still. The boy could see why the cow had not run. Bunched close to her side was a newborn dappled calf.

The elk cow glared angrily at the boy and the pup. She stamped her feet, snorted, and then slowly backed away into the timber, her jaws chomping menacingly. The calf followed awkwardly on spraddled legs, ears flopping, its yellow-and-white-spotted coat lost in splotches of sunlight filtering through the trees. The boy laughed aloud. The elk calf was not at all afraid of him or the dog. The last thing Teddy saw was the calf nudging and butting its mother's flank as they retreated, trying desperately to nurse as it wobbled along.

Teddy slid the rifle back into its boot and swung into the saddle. He called to the hound pup, then swung Concho east out of the park into timber. Spruce and fir grew tall and close. The aspen dwindled to scattered clumps of slender white trunks topped by skimpy tufts of fluttering leaves. The thick carpet of brown needles was soft and springy under the buckskin's hoofs.

A quarter of a mile along Teddy rode out onto a hard-packed game trail and swung Concho east along it, following the curve of the mountain.

Trickles of water seeped down across the trail. Along the edges of the seepages, tracks showed plain on the damp earth. Each time Mark stopped and snuffled noisily over the tracks, his tail beating.

From the saddle Teddy studied the crisscrossed tracks. Some he knew—the deep-cleft heart shape of the deer, the small claw tracks of the porcupine. The padded tracks like those of an overgrown housecat's, he decided, were bobcat. Once there were huge five-toed tracks reaching far out ahead of enormous, rounded pad-marks. The boy's skin tingled. A bear, he was almost certain, and a big one.

They followed the trail spiraling up the side of the mountain for over an hour. In open patches between the trees the boy could see that the sun stood overhead. He began to think about the sandwiches tucked away in his saddlebag.

Suddenly in the distance sounded the muted rush of running water. The buckskin's ears pricked forward. He stepped up his pace.

The dash and slap of water breaking against rock grew louder. As the buckskin topped out over a low ridge,

Teddy gave a sigh of pleasure. Fifty feet ahead, a noisy brook come tumbling down the mountain side, white water surging around low boulders. The trail they were following ended abruptly on the bank of the stream. As Teddy rode up he could see a crisscrossed maze of tracks pocking the bank.

The hound pup waded out into a little backwash pool, pink tongue lapping thirstily. Teddy swung down from the saddle, held onto the reins while Concho sucked and blew his fill. Then he tied the buckskin to a stout aspen and stretched out on his stomach on the bank, shivering as icy water stung his face. Slowly he drank. When he was finished he rolled over on his back, shielding his eyes from the sun with one arm. The hound pup came bounding up, cocked his head, and pawed at Teddy's chest with one forepaw.

Teddy sat up. "Crazy fool pup," he said with a grin. He gave one of Mark's floppy ears a gentle tug, then laid his cheek against the pup's sleek black muzzle for a second. "Crazy fool pup."

He got up then and went over to where Concho was cropping bunch grass under the aspen. Digging the foil-wrapped sandwiches out of the saddlebag, he carried them over to a flat boulder in the shade of a blue spruce. The hound pup followed. Teddy sat down. He peeled back the foil and took out a sandwich. The pup sat down as close against him as he could, brown eyes shining, tongue dripping. Teddy looked from him to the sandwich in his hand and back. Carefully he divided the sandwich into two halves. "I know you're supposed to feed just of an evening," he muttered to the pup, "but this once can't do any harm."

The pup bolted the sandwich down, then watched, tongue lolling, while Teddy finished his half. Teddy divided the second sandwich. "No use begging for more," he told the pup as Mark wolfed his half down, "for that's all there is."

As he spoke there came a soft whisper of wings overhead and a fluffy gray-and-white jay floated down over the spruce and came to a perch atop a nearby boulder. The round black-and-white head cocked first to one side, then to the other. Black button eyes watched the boy and the dog curiously.

Teddy chuckled. He broke off a scrap of crust and tossed it to the camp robber. The jay caught it in mid-air, settled back with a flutter on his perch, and stabbed away at the crust.

The hound pup growled at the bird, then turned around three times and curled up against Teddy's leg, tail to the camp robber.

The jay finished the crust. It spread its wings and flew to perch on the toe of Teddy's boot. Teddy laughed. He broke off a bit of crust and held it out to the bird. A sharp beak snatched it from his fingers. The jay flew back to its perch on the boulder and commenced to eat.

The boy and the jay kept up the game until the last morsel of food was gone. Then the camp robber gave a scolding *cha-cha-cha*, a plaintive *ka-whee-ah*, and spread its wings. Regretfully the boy watched as it vanished over the treetops.

For half an hour the boy and the hound pup sprawled on the boulder in the shade of the spruce. A soft south wind blew down from the snow-capped peak of the mountain. Lazily Teddy watched a brown rock spider scurry in and out of a fissure in the boulder, carrying its white egg-basket under its belly.

All at once the pup's head came up. His nose wrinkled as he sucked in air. Slowly he got to his feet, stood facing the mountain. His hackles rose. A low growl rumbled deep in his throat.

Teddy scrambled to his feet. The boy's heart was pounding. Something was up there on the side of the mountain. He licked his dry lips. Nervously he scanned the timber for any sign of movement. Splotches of sunlight shimmered and danced as the wind bent the trees. Teddy turned, measured the distance to the grazing horse with frightened eyes. He had broken Timothy's cardinal rule. He had left his rifle in the saddle boot.

The hound pup went down off the rock and started up the steep slope with short, choppy steps, head up, nose working. Teddy jumped to the ground, sprinted across to the horse, slid the rifle out of the boot, threw it on ready. Cradling it under his arm, he hurried after the pup.

Mark led the way up through the trees, climbing slowly, favoring his game leg. Every few yards the pup stopped and tested the air, then as if sure resumed the climb.

Teddy slipped and slid as he followed the pup up over rocky outcroppings, across slick stretches of brown needles, under drooping spruce boughs which slapped stingingly at his face. His breath wheezed through his open mouth. Sweat soaked his body.

They reached a scattering of large boulders on the spine of a sharp ridge. Teddy followed the pup in and around through the big rocks. Suddenly they came out onto a rocky shelf. The pup froze. The hair on his neck bristled. Beside him, the boy sucked in his breath in a startled gasp.

Beneath them lay a tiny lake, its water as blue as the sky above. On a strip of sandy beach two hundred feet away stood a great black she-bear, two fat cubs tumbling and scuffling about her feet.

A bellow began to rumble deep in the pup's throat. Teddy dropped his rifle, grabbed the pup's muzzle, choked off the sound.

"Quiet, Mark," he hissed. "Don't make a sound!"

Breath whistled through the boy's nostrils. Cold sweat rolled down his face. He got a firm grip on the pup and knelt down in the lee of a boulder. The bears were upwind from them. They were safe as long as the wind held.

Mark had stopped struggling and was watching the bears with bright eyes. The she-bear was coaxing the cubs down to the water's edge. She led them out along a fallen tree that hung over the lake, close to the water. The cubs followed bravely to the end of the log, but when their mother jumped into the water with a great splash, the cubs clung timidly to the log, woofing with fright.

The she-bear called from the water with a choppy cough, but the cubs clung forlornly to the log. Their mother snorted and grunted. She reared up in the water, sides streaming, and lifted one huge paw menacingly. With frightened squeals the little cubs backed away along the log to the shore, then turned tail and fled up the sandy beach and into a thicket of alders.

The she-bear stalked up out of the lake, shook herself

vigorously, sending water flying, then vanished into the thicket.

The hound pup strained against the boy's hold, whining excitedly.

"Shh, Mark," Teddy whispered, holding the pup tight. "Don't you bark and get that bear mad at us. Shh, now."

The boy crouched there behind the boulder, waiting. He could tell by the tautness of the pup's body that the bears were still in the thicket. Remembering Timothy's warning, he wet a finger and held it up. They were still downwind from the bear and her cubs. Getting a firmer grip on the pup, Teddy settled back to wait.

After a few moments the alders shook, then parted, and the she-bear came shambling down to the shore, the cubs romping after her. The hound pup's hackles rose. There was an angry rumbling in his throat.

"Quiet, boy," Teddy hissed. "Quiet!"

The she-bear had waded out into shallow water. Now her huge head lowered and she drank. The fat black cubs teetered at the water's edge, watching.

The bear gave a short choppy cough and lay down in the water. She raised her head, looked at the cubs on the shore, coughed sharply.

Squealing protestingly the cubs waded out into the lake, lifting their paws high at every step, shaking them until water flew.

Teddy chuckled softly at the comical little fellows. Beside him, the hound pup stood quiet in the circle of his arms, head cocked, eyes watching the cubs.

The cubs reached the she-bear. With loud splashings

they scrambled up onto her back and clung there out of the water.

Carefully the she-bear heaved to her feet, cubs clinging to her fur with excited woofs. Slowly she waded out into deep water. She was swimming, the fat little cubs riding well out of the water.

When the bear was a hundred feet out from shore, Teddy decided it was safe to come out from behind the boulder. He let go his grip on the hound pup and stood up. The she-bear was halfway across the little lake, the cubs riding high on her back.

"Now wasn't that something?" the boy asked the pup, eyes following the swimming bear. "You see how their mama took care of—oh, oh!"

Out in the middle of the lake the she-bear had rolled over deliberately, tossing the little cubs into the water. Now she was swimming rapidly toward the far shore, not even turning her head to look back at the squealing cubs floundering in the water.

"They'll drown!" Teddy cried, but the bear cubs, pointed black snouts sticking up out of the water, were already paddling toward where their mother was coming streaming up out of the lake onto shore. Five minutes later the cubs emerged dripping beside the she-bear. She swung around and led the way up a grassy slope and into the timber.

For the first time since they had come upon the bears, Teddy took a deep breath. He picked up his gun. "Come on, boy," he told the pup. "We're getting out of here."

12

The boy and the hound pup slid and stumbled down the steep slope to the horse. Teddy slipped the rifle into the boot, untied the reins, and climbed into the saddle with a tired sigh. He swung the buckskin around and headed him west toward home, the pup trailing.

For over an hour they followed the switchback game trail lower and lower on the mountain side. Thunderheads gathered around the mountain peaks. The wind blew cold. There was a spattering of raindrops on the trees, but the rain held.

In a thick stand of aspen on a slope above the stream, Teddy came upon huge drifts of columbine. The big blue-and-white blossoms tossed in the breeze on thread-like stems. The boy reined up. Just yesterday his aunt had been yearning aloud for columbine clumps for the rocky slope back of the cabin. If he could take her some plants, she would be pleased. He studied the delicate blossoms, chewing thoughtfully on his bottom lip, pondering how to carry them so they would not wilt.

After a moment he swung to the ground. He tied Concho to an aspen, then set off down through an outcropping of rock to where the stream churned noisily around upjutting boulders in its race to the canyon below.

On a punky stump at the water's edge he found what he wanted—a thick blanket of spongy green moss. Carefully he peeled off a large slab, and holding it across the palms of his hands, climbed back up to the columbine. Kneeling, he spread the moss out on the turf.

He climbed back down to the stream. With his pocketknife he cut long mountain-willow wands and carried them up to where he had placed the moss. From a large aspen he peeled off two slabs of bark. One slab he bent into a shallow cylinder, boring holes with his knife through the double layer of bark at the overlap. He peeled a willow wand and laced the bark together.

The hound pup crowded up close and nosed the cylinder.

"Careful, boy," Teddy warned. "Don't you break it." He turned the second slab of bark with sappy side up as he spoke, placed the cylinder in the center, and laboriously cut a crude circle around it, leaving ample overlap. Then he bored holes around both and laced the bottom slab on securely. He sat back when he was finished and proudly surveyed the crude container.

"When I was learning to make bark baskets in crafts at school, I sure never thought I'd be making one out here in Colorado," he told the pup with a grin. "Now I'll line it with moss and dig up the plants with plenty of dirt around the roots. That way, I'll get them home to Aunt Pat without them wilting."

He was tamping dirt securely around the plants bedded in the basket when the pup barked. Teddy sat back on his heels. The pup stood stiff-legged, facing the back trail. Teddy listened. A horse was coming.

The boy scrambled to his feet just as Timothy rode in sight on the trail. "Timothy!" he shouted gladly.

The old man raised a hand in greeting. A moment later he reined up beside the boy and swung to the ground. His keen blue eye studied the container of flowers. "Not bad," he grunted, "not bad at all."

"I made the basket with my dad's pocketknife," the boy said eagerly. "I've had it since—since—" Teddy's voice faltered. He swallowed. "They're for Aunt Pat," he said after a moment. "I'm sure glad to see you, Timothy. I've got lots to tell you."

Timothy looked at the boy quizzically. "Ever see an elk calf, lad?" he asked abruptly. "An honest-to-goodness newborn elk calf?"

"Why, we saw one just today," the boy cried, brown eyes sparkling. "It was up on—"

"You're looking a mite peaked," the old man cut in

flatly. "Didn't you fetch your dinner along? You wouldn't be sharing your grub with the pup here, would you, or tossing it to the birds, say?"

"I did give part of my sandwiches to Mark," the boy stammered, "and there was this camp robber, see—" His voice trailed off. He stood staring at the old man.

"And what do we do if we stumble onto a sow bear with cubs?" Timothy continued relentlessly.

"We get out as fast as we can," the boy stammered. "Only this time was different. This time I didn't know till—Timothy! How do you know every single thing me and Mark did today?"

Timothy's good blue eye twinkled. He rumpled the boy's brown hair gently. "You didn't think old Timothy was going to send his partner out on the mountains without trailing along to see no harm comes, did you?"

Teddy stared at him openmouthed. "I don't believe you," he stammered. "I never once saw—Mark would have smelled you if—"

Timothy grinned. "Didn't you? Would he? Don't you be forgetting, lad, old Timothy was a mountain man years before you were ever born. I've trailed many a grizzly all day through timber without him ever knowing. Any time I can't outsmart a couple of pups like you and Mark, it's time for me to quit."

A reluctant grin creased the boy's face. "Aw, Timothy," he muttered weakly, then broke off, face reddening. "Then you saw what I forgot there where we ate our dinner," he said ashamedly. "I forgot and left my gun in the saddle boot."

Timothy nodded. "It was your one blunder," he said soberly, "and a bad one. I won't always be watching over you, lad. Today was sort of a test. I don't want you ever to forget your gun again, Teddy. It could well mean the difference between you living and dying out here in the wilderness."

"I won't, Timothy," the boy said earnestly. "I won't ever forget again."

The old man held out his hand. The boy took it. They shook hands solemnly.

"Well, now that's settled," Timothy said briskly, "you get on your horse and I'll hand up the posies to you. We'd best light out for home. If I know your Aunt Pat, she'll be pacing the floor till you come in sight, safe and sound."

Only she was not. They rode upon her suddenly around a sharp curve in the trail. She had reined the black stallion up and sat watching the trail expectantly.

"I heard you coming," she said relievedly. "Teddy, I'm sorry. I must be getting old. I couldn't do a thing all day but worry. If only I'd known Timothy had decided to go with you—"

"I didn't know myself," the boy told her, giving Timothy a reproachful look. "I didn't even know he was trailing me till about five minutes ago."

Patricia looked at Timothy.

"Now, Pat," the old man said testily, "you didn't think I was fool enough to turn the lad loose in the mountains without seeing how he made out."

Patricia smiled grimly. "I thought you'd lost your mind," she told him. "Teddy, the columbine—they're lovely. And what a clever basket to carry them in."

The boy's face reddened. "They're for you, Aunt Pat. You said yesterday you wanted some."

After that day Teddy took the hound pup out whenever Timothy was free to come with them. Under the old man's patient guidance the boy began to learn the secrets of the timber—learned where wild raspberries hid, red and juicy-sweet under short-stemmed leaves, learned the deep, green pools below shallow rapids in Thunder River where speckled trout lurked in shadows, learned the big, splayed pad-marks of the mountain lion in crumbly duff in dark reaches of the forest.

The boy grew in nature like corn in the night. The hound pup's leg suppled. Day by day the old man and the boy and the pup ranged farther and farther.

August came. The days were dry and hot. Thunderheads gathered around the mountain peaks each afternoon, but no rain fell. Timothy took to watching the sky. Worry lurked in his good blue eye.

"Timber's getting dry as tinder," he fumed to the boy during the second week of August. "I don't like the looks of things, not one bit. Look at the mountains. See how the spruce and the pine and the aspen are wilting."

"Aunt Pat says it always rains in August," the boy protested. "Why are you worrying so, Timothy? There's still plenty of water in the streams."

"Water in the streams, aye," the old man said. "That's not my worry, lad. There's only one thing here in my mountains I fear. Fire."

The first post card came for Teddy that week. It had been mailed in Albuquerque. It was a picture of Indians dancing. On the back Clarence had written in his big sprawling hand:

Trip fine. Heap big Injuns here. Headed for Disneyland. Chin up, Fatso.

Clarence

Teddy showed the post card to his aunt, then propped it on the mantel in the living room under the mounted head of the great black bear. Patricia would see him stop sometimes, stand gazing at the post card, his face expressionless.

"Did you ever answer his letter?" she burst out one day when she caught Teddy standing before the mantel.

The boy shook his head. He looked at her, his brown eyes troubled. "I meant to, honest. I even started a letter one night—but I got to thinking about my dad—" The boy broke off, swallowing hard. "I just kept putting it off."

The second post card arrived a week later. It was a picture of Disneyland.

Having fine time. Sure wish you were here.

Clarence

Teddy propped the second card beside the first. When Timothy rode down next afternoon, Patricia showed him the cards. Timothy read them carefully, studied the pictures, put the cards back on the mantel. He said nothing.

The days passed. The drought worsened. Patricia took to turning on the radio morning and afternoon, listening to the local news. The forest rangers had issued fire warnings. Campfires were forbidden. Day after day a ranger's voice droned its warning to tourists. No fires of any kind. No cigarette butts tossed out of car windows.

The third week in August, Timothy appeared early one morning. Patricia and Teddy and the pup came out on the deck to meet him. Timothy climbed the steps wearily.

"That blasted black bear's been at my cabin up on Lobo again," he told them disgustedly. "Rode up there yesterday with an elk hunter from Detroit. He wanted to see the terrain he'd be hunting this fall. I'd left the cabin door wide open. Figured if the bear could walk in and see there wasn't any grub in the cabin, he'd leave things alone. The blasted varmint hadn't even used the door. Tore a big hole in the roof and went in that way."

"I'm sorry, Timothy," Pat said sympathetically.

"What are you going to do now?" Teddy asked eagerly. "I could help you patch up the hole, Timothy."

The old man shook his head. "If you really want to help me, lad, you can ride up and milk Anabel this evening. I'm going up right away and patch up the roof. Aim to sleep up there in the cabin tonight. May be that my bear friend'll come back, and I can come to terms with him."

Teddy shivered at the old man's tone. "I'll be glad to milk for you, Timothy," he said disappointedly, "and I'll feed the hounds. Don't you worry about a thing."

The old man's face lighted. "Mighty nice to have a partner you can depend on," he told the boy.

"I hate for you to stay alone so far up in the mountains," Patricia said worriedly.

Timothy turned, gazed up at the snow-patched peaks

towering high above the canyon. "A man's never alone in the mountains, Pat," he said slowly. "Not a man who knows them and loves them. Don't you worry. I'll be back at my cabin by noon tomorrow, whether my bear friend shows up or not."

13

At four o'clock that afternoon, Teddy and Patricia saddled the horses and started up the trail to Timothy's. They took Mark along.

"I still wish Timothy had let me go up to the camp cabin with him," Teddy fumed as they jogged along. "I could have handed him things and stuff."

"He didn't want you there if the bear comes," she said absently. "A bear that'll deliberately tear up a cabin twice, and for no reason, is apt to be a mean one. Besides,"—she glanced up at the sky—"Timothy was certain we're in for a storm. He told me so."

Teddy looked at the sky uneasily. The sun shone bright. The wind felt hot and dry. "You're worried, aren't you?" he asked. "About Timothy, I mean?"

"Yes, I am," she said frankly. "Timothy's not young any more. He takes risks he shouldn't take."

The hounds in the pen welcomed them with noisy bellows. The cabin door was unlocked. Teddy took down the milk pail from the shelf, rinsed it out with water from the kettle simmering on the back of the range. He found a clean, white milk rag in a drawer, wet it, and wrung it out.

"I'll feed the hounds while you're milking," Patricia told him. "Timothy's left the cereal and meat in the dishpan here."

Teddy started down the worn trail past the dog pen, the hound pup trotting by his side. The hounds followed along inside the fence to the end, barking excitedly. The Jersey cow Anabel waited at the corral gate, placidly chewing her cud. Teddy and the pup eased inside. The Jersey followed them into the barn and stood waiting at the feed trough while Teddy measured out oats into the feed bucket.

The boy poured the feed in the trough, fetched a milk stool, and sat down beside the cow. Carefully he washed off her bag with the wet cloth, ducking her tail as it switched placidly.

"Hold still, Anabel," he said sternly, pressing his head against her flank.

He began to milk. The steady squish and squirt of milk into pail made a gentle rhythm. The boy glanced sideways at the hound pup sitting a few feet away, his head cocked, tongue lolling, and melancholy eyes watching the jets of milk. He smiled.

The hounds paid them no heed when the boy carried the pail of milk back up past the pen. He could hear their muted grunts as they rooted in the feed troughs. In the cabin his aunt had a milk crock and straining cloth ready. Carefully the boy poured the milk, taking his time, letting the strainer empty before pouring more. When he was finished, Patricia stored the crock in the refrigerator. They washed the milk pail and rinsed out the cloths in hot water.

"Guess that's everything," Patricia said when they were finished. She glanced about the neat cabin. "Ready, Teddy?"

They paused for a moment on the slope before they mounted the horses. It was very still in the canyon. The sunlight seemed pale. Not a breeze stirred the limp spruce boughs. Teddy looked up at the mountains. Over the peaks the sky was black and forbidding. Thunderheads boiled ominously. Lightning rippled dully through the massed clouds. The boy shivered.

They reached home in time for the six o'clock news. Patricia switched on the radio in the living room. There was the noisy crackling of static, then the drone of a man's voice.

"—for this vicinity, severe thunderstorms tonight and possibly tomorrow. I repeat, severe thunderstorms tonight and tomorrow."

Patricia switched off the radio. "I could have told him that," she muttered. "Well, let's go see what we can find to eat for supper, Teddy."

Before they went to bed at ten, Patricia and Teddy went out onto the deck for a look at the sky. Overhead, stars twinkled brightly. Along the rim of the canyon, lightning rippled palely from peak to peak. The air was oppressively still.

The storm broke at midnight, broke with a blue-white flash of lightning that lit up the canyon, a thunderclap that jarred the cabin.

Teddy sprang bolt upright out of his bunk. The hound pup jumped to the floor with an uneasy whine. The boy's heart was pounding. Flash after flash of lightning crackled around the cabin. There was the pungent smell of sulphur in the air. The cabin shuddered under jarring claps of thunder.

By the weird flashes of lightning the boy felt his way to the door, the pup at his heels. He stumbled across the little hall and flung open the door to his aunt's bedroom. Patricia turned from the window where she stood watching the storm.

"I'm scared," the boy panted, teeth chattering.

His aunt crossed to him swiftly and put an arm around his trembling body. "We'll be all right," she told him soothingly. "If lightning strikes, it'll hit a tree. They're so much taller than the cabin. We'll be all right, honey."

Lightning flared and thunder crashed. All at once there came the spatter of rain on the roof.

"Now it'll get better," Patricia said soothingly. "It's raining. Now it'll get better."

Rain beat on the roof. The flashes of lightning came farther and farther apart, died out with a last weak stroke.

The thunder receded, muttering dully along the rim of the canyon.

Only then did Patricia release her hold on the boy. "Come sleep with me the rest of the night," she told him. "There's plenty of room for us both in my bunk. But Mark will have to sleep on the floor."

Teddy snuggled down under the blanket with a weary sigh. "I never was so scared in my whole life," he murmured drowsily. "I kept thinking about Timothy, up there in the camp cabin by himself. Do you think Timothy was afraid of the—" the boy's voice trailed off. He was asleep.

Beside him his aunt lay staring into the darkness, glad that the boy had fallen asleep before she had had time to answer him. Timothy's camp cabin was in big timber. The old man had been afraid of a fire. He'd said only that morning that the timber was as dry as tinder, said you could smell the resin oozing from trees. Patricia bit her lip. The rain had already stopped. Lightning like they'd had tonight played havoc with dry timber.

There came a sudden thud, a heavy weight across her feet, a deliberate milling around, a warm mound against her legs. Patricia grinned wryly in the dark. The hound pup had come to bed.

They overslept next morning. The hound pup woke them up.

"Look how bright the sun's shining," Teddy yawned. "Wonder how long it rained."

"Not long enough," his aunt replied. "Better put on your robe, Teddy, and take the pup outside. I'll get the coffee on."

She was already in the kitchen when she heard the boy scream: "Aunt Pat! Aunt Pat!"

She raced across the living room and out onto the deck. Teddy stood by the rail, staring up toward Timothy's place. The boy's face was white. His eyes were big and terrified.

Patricia whirled, and let out a cry of dismay. A heavy pall of gray smoke spread in a long, horizontal wall close up under timber line on Arrowhead Peak, just east of Lobo Mountain.

She dashed into the living room and ran back out with binoculars. She focused them on the smoke.

"What can you see?" Teddy cried. "What can you see?"

She handed him the glasses. "Turn that little center focus wheel till it comes clear."

The boy adjusted the glasses. He sucked in his breath. "I can see fire licking clear up to the top of the pines," he stammered, lowering the glasses and looking at her with terrified eyes.

"The storm last night," she said flatly. "Lightning must have struck a tree up there under Arrowhead Peak. Timothy kept saying the timber was as dry as tinder."

"Timothy!" the boy cried. "Timothy's up there!"

"Not on Arrowhead, Teddy. Timothy's camp cabin is over on Lobo."

"But Lobo's right next to Arrowhead," the boy said fearfully. He licked a finger and held it up. "The wind's out of the south. That'll keep the fire from spreading onto Lobo, won't it?"

"Unless the wind shifts," she said grimly.

"If the wind shifts, Timothy's likely to get cut off by the fire up there!" The boy was on the verge of tears.

"Chances are Timothy's got out long before now," Patricia reassured him. "Timothy's a mountain man. He knows more about forest fires than most. You know he's been fretting over the danger of a fire for weeks now."

"Just the same, I want to go up to his cabin and see if he's back," the boy cried. "Let's saddle the horses and go right now."

She wavered for a moment, but the terror in Teddy's eyes decided her. "Get dressed. We'll ride up."

They started out up the highway at a lope, the hound pup running ahead of the horses. A quarter of a mile up the road three jeeps passed them with loud honks. Men packed in the jeeps waved.

"Fire fighters," Patricia told Teddy. "On their way up to Forest Service Headquarters."

"Where is the Headquarters?"

"Five miles on beyond the Post."

They reached the fork in the road, swung onto the rutted tracks up Columbine Canyon.

"You think those fire fighters can put out the fire?" Teddy asked worriedly.

"They'll put it out. Those men have been fighting timber fires for years, most of them. You remember Timothy pointed out that Forest Service watchtower to you the day we drove over to the Post, Teddy. There are towers like that all through the mountains. At the first puff of smoke, the watcher on the tower telephones to Headquarters and gives the location. The dispatcher alerts the fire fighters, gives them their assignments."

"How long does it take them?" the boy asked. "To put out a forest fire, I mean?"

"That depends," she said slowly, "depends on how accessible the fire is."

"What does that mean?"

"How rough the terrain is, whether there are roads leading up anywhere near, what kind of machinery they can get close enough to fight the fire."

Teddy licked his lips nervously. "Are there any roads up on Arrowhead and Lobo?" he asked.

His aunt shook her head. "Not any, Teddy. They'll have to use the parachute fighters."

"Look, Aunt Pat, through that gap in the timber there. The fire's getting over closer to Lobo."

"Wind's shifted around to the north," she said shortly, "that's why. There's the cabin. Can you tell if Timothy's back yet?"

Teddy stood up in the stirrups. "I don't see Maud out front," he said nervously, "and she's not in the corral."

Patricia glanced at her wrist watch. "Ten o'clock," she muttered. "His not being home doesn't really mean anything yet."

"Where is Timothy's camp cabin, Aunt Pat?"

"About a mile up and east from Sky Lake, where you saw the bears," she replied.

They forded the stream and started up the slope. The hound pup streaked ahead, barking as he neared the cabin. The hounds in the pen began to clamor. Mark was scratching on the cabin door when Patricia and Teddy dismounted at the hitching rail.

"Look at Mark," Teddy said nervously. "He acts like he knows something's wrong."

The pup bounded down off the step, crowding against the boy's legs, whining uneasily.

Patricia did not answer. She stood gazing up at the ominous wall of smoke billowing around Arrowhead Peak. One hand fumbled for the binocular case slung over her shoulder. She took out the glasses and raised them to her eyes.

"How does it look now?" Teddy asked apprehensively.

Wordlessly she handed him the glasses. He focused. "It's—" He broke off, lowered the glasses. "Listen! I hear a plane."

"I hear it, too," his aunt said. "Must be the Forest Service spotter plane."

The singing whine of a single engine grew louder and louder. A moment later a small orange plane came skimming low over the treetops up the canyon from the west, dipped its wings over the cabin, faded smaller and smaller over the timber toward the smoke pall.

"That's Cleve Parks," Patricia told the boy. "Cleve's the dispatcher, the one who decides where to drop the parachute fighters into timber."

"I bet the parachute fighters will put the fire out right away," the boy said hopefully.

"Let's say a little prayer they can," Patricia replied soberly. She glanced at her watch. "Ten thirty," she murmured. "Teddy, would you be afraid to stay here alone for a couple of hours?"

"Why?" the boy asked, startled.

"Just in case Timothy should happen to ride in while I'm gone."

"But where are you going?"

"To get the jeep and drive over to the Post. I can telephone Forest Service Headquarters from there, let them know Timothy's up on Lobo."

The boy's lip began to tremble. "You think something's happened to Timothy," he stammered.

She looked him straight in the eye. "I'm not going to lie to you, Teddy. With a fire spreading over Arrowhead, Timothy ought to be down off Lobo by now. Maybe Maud's had an accident. Maybe Timothy has. I don't know what, but something's happened to him."

"But why can't we ride up and see?" the boy cried. "You know where the camp cabin is."

"Because if the wind holds out of the north, that fire's going to jump over on Lobo in no time," she said flatly. "Will you be afraid alone, Teddy?"

"Not with Mark here, and the other dogs," he said stoutly.

She gave him a quick hug. "Good boy. I'll hurry," she promised. "I'll hurry like everything. Here, take the binocular case. I'll leave the glasses, so you can watch the fire."

"What are you going to tell them at headquarters?" the boy cried as she swung into the saddle.

"Tell them to fly in a helicopter and find Timothy." She swung the stallion around. "I'll hurry, Teddy."

The boy watched forlornly as she sent the stallion across the stream and down the rutted road at a gallop.

"She never would even lope Diablo on that road before," he muttered to the pup as horse and rider vanished into the trees. "Listen, Mark, the spotter plane's coming back. Hear it?"

He clapped the glasses to his eyes and swung them along the line of smoke. There was the orange plane. It seemed to be coming straight out of the cloud of smoke. It was veering to the north. Disappointedly he followed it with the glasses until it vanished behind a mountain. Slowly he lowered the glasses and walked over and sat down on the cabin step. The pup followed him, sat down against his legs.

Teddy reached out and stroked the pup's sleek black head. "A mile up and east from Sky Lake," he muttered. "That makes the cabin a good six miles from here."

The pup whined, looked up at the boy with sad eyes. Teddy tugged gently at one silken black ear. "She said in a couple of hours," he told the pup, "but it'll take her a couple of hours to get to the Post. A fellow on a good horse like Concho could get up to the camp cabin in less time than that."

He glanced at his wrist watch. "Eleven o'clock," he told the pup. He raised the glasses and studied the billowing wall of smoke. Writhing tongues of flame leaped up against the gray. "It's lots closer to Lobo," the boy muttered.

Slowly he lowered the glasses. He looked at Concho standing placidly at the hitching rail, looked back up at the billowing smoke on the mountain. He swallowed convulsively. His aunt had not actually told him to stay here at the cabin, but he knew in his heart that she had meant him to. He just couldn't. Not with Timothy maybe needing him up there on the mountain.

He slid the binoculars into the case and slung the strap over his head. Kneeling down, he put both arms around the hound pup. "I'm going after Timothy," he said thickly. "I'm scared, but I'm going. I'm not taking you, Mark. You might get hurt. I couldn't stand you getting hurt again. I'm going to tie you to the hitching rail. You've got to understand, boy, why I'm leaving you. I just couldn't stand it if you got hurt again."

14

Leaving the pup on the step, Teddy hurried into the cabin. He took down a canteen from a wall peg and filled it from the water bucket in the sink. He went over to the guns racked on the wall. Timothy had taken the .270. Teddy plucked down the .30-30. In a cupboard drawer he found boxes of cartridges. He opened the box of .30-30's, loaded the rifle, and stuffed half a dozen extras into his shirt pockets. A bowie knife in its leather scabbard lay next to the cartridges. The boy snatched it up, clipped the scabbard to his belt.

From a wall peg he jerked down a coiled lariat. He stood holding rifle and rope, eyes darting about the cabin. "Another rope to tie Mark with," he muttered aloud.

He carried his gear outside. He looked up at the mountains. Cold sweat popped out over his body. The fire was eating its way around Arrowhead toward Lobo. Great billowing clouds of smoke rolled up high into the sky, blotting out Arrowhead Peak.

Mark rubbed against the boy's legs, whining.

"It's all right, fellow," Teddy murmured, carrying his gear over to his horse. He slipped the rifle into the saddle boot, tied the lariat to the saddle, and slung the strap of the canteen over the horn. He hurried back into the cabin and brought out a coil of slender rope. He knelt down beside the pup. His hands shook as he tied one end of the rope securely to Mark's collar. Mark whined uneasily, biting at the rope.

"You've got to be good, Mark," the boy pleaded, putting both arms around the pup, holding him tight. "You've got to be good, for Timothy."

The pup pulled free. He began to lick the boy's face. Teddy got to his feet, looped the rope over the hitching rail, tied a stout slipknot. The pup reared up against him, forepaws on Teddy's chest, tail beating. Teddy hugged the pup to him. Tears blurred his eyes.

"You be a good boy now," he choked. "I'll be back for you, just as soon as I find Timothy."

He turned, fumbled Concho's reins up, climbed into the saddle. The hound pup stood gazing up at him forlornly, making soft whimpering noises.

Teddy swung the buckskin away, dug his heels in, sent him at a lope down to the stream. The hound pup let out a high, drawn-out wail. The hounds in the pen began to bark.

Concho splashed through the stream. Teddy swung him left up the far bank. Behind him the baying of the hounds slowly faded and died.

Trees towered tall and green on both sides of the wide, beaten trail, hiding the smoke from the forest fire. Teddy glanced at the stream. It was running low, chuckling and churning down around upjutting boulders.

The buckskin settled down into a ground-eating walk. As they climbed, the boy gazed about, chewing on his lip. The timber seemed different somehow. It came to him suddenly as the buckskin's hoofs rang on rock. There were no birds singing in the trees. The timber stretched away silent, deserted. Teddy swallowed. The forest had become a lonely place.

The trail steepened. The buckskin strained against the incline. High overhead, wind soughed through tall pines. Teddy twisted around in the saddle, glanced back down the trail. Puffs of dust rolled back from under Concho's hoofs. The boy shivered. Dry as tinder.

They reached the fork in the trail at last. The boy swung the buckskin up the right fork toward Lobo Mountain. Concho climbed stolidly. He did not even prick his ears when a rabbit bounded across the trail almost under his feet and vanished down the mountain side.

They passed the spread of columbine under the aspen. The flowers had already felt the first night frosts of autumn. The blossoms hung shriveled and brown.

The trail steepened. The labored breathing of the

horse sounded loud in the stillness. As they topped out over a rocky ridge and into a little park, Teddy reined up to give Concho a breather.

Giant pines rimmed the clearing. High above the tops of the pines, great clouds of brown-tinged smoke billowed and swirled around Arrowhead Peak. The boy licked his lips nervously. For the first time, he was afraid.

All at once he heard the faraway hum of a plane. Eagerly he searched the sky. At last he spotted it, a silver speck flashing in sunlight away to the north. He watched it, his heart pounding. The plane loomed larger and larger, a big C-47.

Suddenly the plane banked, swung away to the east in a wide circle. Teddy fumbled the binoculars out of their case and raised them to his eyes. The plane was flying low over Arrowhead. Smoke hid it for a moment. Now it was swinging back around toward Lobo, was gaining altitude.

Three times the plane circled above the smoke clouds. Then it went into a steep climb. Teddy followed it with the glasses. Now it was high over Arrowhead. Suddenly a black speck plummeted down from the plane, then another, and another. A parachute mushroomed out, then a second, and a third. The boy watched breathlessly as they floated down and vanished behind smoke and treetops.

The plane was circling Arrowhead again. Three parachutes blossomed out under it, one after another. Now the plane was banking, straightening out, flying away to the north. Slowly Teddy lowered the glasses. He stared dully at the smoke clouds. The parachute fighters had all been dropped close to the fire over on Arrowhead. If the fire reached Lobo, they would be of no help to Timothy.

Teddy rammed the glasses into the case and sent Concho at a gallop across the park. The trail beyond was rocky and steep. The buckskin dropped to a walk. Breath whistled through his nostrils. Sweat streaked his withers.

A mile farther on, they rounded a bend and rode out into a clearing. Teddy knew it at once. It was where he had shared his lunch with Mark and the camp robber.

He watered Concho at a little pool between two boulders at the edge of the stream. As the horse drank, the boy sat studying the rocky ridge he and Mark had climbed to reach Sky Lake. He knew he could not possibly take Concho up over those rocks. They would have to follow the trail around up through timber to the lake.

He was still staring up at the ridge when he heard the birds, a faint, faraway chirping and twittering from high overhead. He looked up. Silhouetted darkly against gray clouds, hundreds of birds were winging westward across the sky. Teddy swallowed hard. The birds were leaving the mountain.

He touched the horse with his heels, sent him splashing across the little stream and out onto the wide, beaten trail beyond. The trail climbed steeply, zigzagging around boulders and bushy spruce. They topped out around the end of the ridge onto the timbered shore of Sky Lake.

The surface of the lake rippled dull and gray. Suddenly Teddy felt the wind. It blew warm and ugly straight out of the east. The boy's heart thudded. Fire would come riding that east wind, would come roaring and leaping across the timbered canyon between Arrowhead and Lobo.

He kicked Concho into a gallop down the trail along the shore of the lake. Hot wind tore at his face. Trees faded past in a grayed blur.

Sky Lake was behind them. Concho slowed on the steep trail up the mountain side. Teddy's heart was hammering. The camp cabin could not be far away.

Suddenly through the trees on the left, the boy saw a small band of elk bucks. They came noiselessly, came in a fast, high-stepping walk down through the trees, small, long heads held out straight, great velvet-clad antlers laid back on brown shoulders. Then they were gone without a sound down the mountain side.

Teddy shivered. He peered frantically through the trees for sight of the cabin. He caught a swift movement ahead to the left of the trail. He squinted, trying to see. Suddenly he made them out, a great band of mule deer, does and fawns and bucks, bounding down through the trees, bunched feet scarcely touching turf as they streamed across the trail and faded down the mountain.

"They know the fire's coming," the boy whispered. "They're getting out. Everything's getting out."

The trail bent sharply to the right around a great dead pine. As Concho rounded the bend he snorted in fright, shied wildly. Teddy grabbed for the saddle horn. His mouth dropped open. Loping straight down the trail toward them came a gaunt gray wolf, jaws gaping, tongue hanging. Teddy fought the horse to a stop beside the trail. He grabbed his gun. Before he had it out of the boot the wolf sped past, vanished around the bend.

Teddy shoved the gun back with shaking hands. He raked the buckskin with his heels, sending him pounding up the trail.

A small park opened up in the timber. Teddy sent the horse across at a gallop. On the far side he reined up. The trail forked. One fork led straight ahead. The other angled off to the left.

"The one straight ahead," Teddy muttered aloud. "That's heading due—" he broke off, raised his head, sniffed. His heart lurched. There was the acrid smell of smoke in the air. The boy looked up. Heavy clouds of gray smoke were scudding across the sky.

At that moment there came a loud crashing noise in the timber ahead, the terrified snorting of an animal. Teddy grabbed out his gun, thumbed back the hammer. Suddenly a big mule deer buck came staggering out through the trees, stumbling, ramming against tree trunks. One velveted antler dangled broken. Chest and shoulders were seared and bloody.

Concho whinnied in terror. With a panicked snort the buck wheeled, sprang away, crashed headlong into the trunk of a big pine, fell.

Teddy was breathing in shallow gasps. He swung to the ground and tied the horse to a pine. Gripping the rifle against his chest, he eased over to the fallen buck. Hot sickness welled up in him as he stared down at the heaving flanks, the charred chest and shoulders. The buck had been blinded by the fire.

The boy sobbed aloud. He put the muzzle of the rifle

against the buck's head, squeezed the trigger. The shot rang out. The buck jerked convulsively, lay still.

Blindly the boy turned away. He levered a cartridge into the chamber, shoved the gun back into the saddle boot. As he reached for the reins, the faint, faraway singing bay of a hound wafted up from below on the mountain side. The boy froze. He held his breath, straining to hear. The baying came again, high and sweet, closer now, louder, louder. The boy whirled.

"Mark!" he shouted. "Mark!"

15

The hound pup came catapulting out of the timber. The clearing rang with his baying. He was across in a blurred streak of gray, was all over the boy, barking, licking at his face, tail beating frenziedly.

Teddy grabbed the wriggling pup to him. He glimpsed the chewed-off rope end dangling from Mark's collar. "Crazy fool dog," the boy sobbed. "Oh, Mark, Mark, we've got to hurry! We've got to find Timothy!"

He let go of the pup, untied the horse, climbed into

the saddle. "Come on, boy," he shouted, swinging Concho up the trail straight east.

The hound pup raced after the horse for a few yards. All at once the pup stopped, feet planted. He pointed his nose in the air, let out a high, drawn-out wail.

Teddy reined up. "Come on, boy. It's all right."

The pup did not budge. Again he wailed.

"Oh, Mark," Teddy groaned, "don't go balky on me now." He wheeled the horse around, rode back. "It's all right, boy," he called soothingly, "come—"

But the hound pup had whirled, was racing back toward the clearing, his excited voice rolling back.

"The other trail!" Teddy cried. "He's trying to tell me! The other trail!"

He kicked the buckskin into a run back to the clearing. The hound pup was already away up the left fork. Teddy sent the horse pounding after him.

Concho followed the wildly barking pup through a thick stand of aspen, down and up out of a shallow ravine, around a wide curving bend, out into a smoke-filled clearing. Through the haze of smoke Teddy glimpsed the small log cabin on the far side, the log shed beside it. Over the barking of the hound pup he caught the shrill whinny of Timothy's dun mare.

Teddy reined Concho to a sliding stop before the cabin. The door was open. The hound pup was already racing around to the back, barking frantically.

Teddy flung himself out of the saddle. "Timothy!" he called. He tied the horse to an aspen with shaking hands, raced around the corner of the cabin. "Timothy!"

The hound pup's head was buried in the bushy boughs of a huge pine that lay fallen out into the clearing. Teddy caught one glimpse of the splintered, jagged stump. Then he was squirming in among the twisted branches. "Timothy!" he screamed.

Timothy lay on his back, his good eye closed, a trickle of blood on his forehead. A huge forked limb pinned him to the ground.

"Timothy!" Teddy choked, squirming under a heavy branch to the old man's side. "Timothy!"

The old man's eye opened. "Good lad," he mumbled dazedly. "Good lad."

"We've got to get you out of here," the boy sobbed. "The fire's coming! Tell me what to do, Timothy!"

Timothy's eye focused sharply. His face came alive. "You're not alone!" he cried.

"Aunt Pat's gone for the helicopter," the boy hiccoughed. "What happened, Timothy?"

"Last night," the old man panted. "Lightning. Tree pinned me down. Get out from here, Teddy!"

"Tell me what to do!" the boy cried.

"Get out!" the old man shouted. "Turn Maud loose and get out! The fire's already on Lobo! It'll come like the wind. Get out!"

Teddy looked at the old man levelly. "Tell me what to do," he repeated quietly. "I'm not getting out."

For a long moment they looked at each other. Timothy's Adam's apple bobbed as he swallowed. "The saw," he said after a moment, "get the saw from the cabin."

Teddy squirmed out between the heavy branches. With Mark at his heels, he raced around to the front of the cabin, grabbed up the saw inside the door. He ran over to Concho, snatched the canteen off the saddle, raced back around to the toppled tree. Awkwardly he squirmed through the branches to the old man. He laid the saw down, unscrewed the cap of the canteen, lifted Timothy's head, and held the canteen to his lips.

Timothy drank deeply. The water gave him new life. "The fork of the limb nearest you," he said calmly. "If you can saw it through, I can get out."

Teddy picked up the saw. "It won't hurt your chest?" he asked anxiously. "I mean, the limb's pressing so tight."

"I can stand it," Timothy said grimly. "There's no time, lad."

Teddy laid the saw across the limb.

"Now take it easy like," Timothy cautioned. "Let the sharp-edged teeth do the work. If you make hard work of it, we'll never get me out."

Teddy took a firm grip on the saw handle. The saw bit into the soft wood.

"Push easy," Timothy cautioned, "pull easy. Get a rhythm. That's it. Swing your body to it. Easy now, don't let it buckle. Push, pull, easy now."

The saw bit through the wood. Sweat rolled down the boy's face. His arm began to throb. He bit hard at his lip. Across and back, across and back. Sweat soaked his body. He blinked smarting eyes. The smoke was getting bad.

"Rest," Timothy said sharply.

Teddy slumped to the ground. His arm was jerking. Panting, he massaged it. "Got to keep going," he gasped. "I'm not half through the limb."

"You'll go faster for a rest," Timothy told him. "Listen!" He raised his head.

Above the pounding of his heart Teddy heard. It was

a dull roar, coming from out of the east. He scrambled to his knees. His heart lurched. Through the smoke haze he saw red tongues of flame leaping between the trees.

"It's the fire," Timothy said quietly. He looked at the boy. "We'll never make it, Teddy. You've got to mind me, lad. Take the horses and the pup and get out."

Teddy did not answer him. He took a firm grip on the saw handle. He began to saw.

"I told you to leave off and get out!" Timothy barked. Then he caught himself and added quietly: "I'm an old man. My life's lived. Your whole life's before you, lad. Get out!"

"I'm not going," Teddy said grimly, pushing the saw smoothly through the wood. "I'm half through the limb. We'll get out."

"Dear God," the old man whispered. His head dropped back. A tear trembled at the corner of his eye.

Back and forth went the saw. The hound pup milled up and down along the toppled pine, whining. The roar of the fire was louder now. The tethered horses whinnied shrilly. The wind was a hot blast out of the east. Stinging sweat poured off the boy's forehead, blinding him. He swiped at it with grimy sleeve. Back and forth went the saw.

A burning branch blew into the clearing on the wind. Out of the corner of his eye Teddy watched where it fell, watched while it flared briefly, then sputtered, smoking. While he watched there came a loud crashing through the trees to the east, and a huge black bear raced out across the clearing, a living torch. The next moment it was gone down the mountain.

Nausea welled up in the boy. He clenched his teeth

tight. Back and forth went the saw. Almost through, almost through. His arm was one throbbing, searing pain. There was a trickle of blood on his lip where his teeth had bitten down hard. Back and forth, back and forth. Then the saw leaped in his hand. There came a thud. The limb came free.

Teddy dropped the saw. Frantically he tugged the limb off Timothy's chest. The old man was squirming, struggling. The boy clamped his hands under Timothy's armpits. "Can you get up?" he panted.

"Ribs smashed," Timothy gasped. "Help me out."

The boy's breath was whistling through his teeth. He clawed the branches apart, half dragged Timothy out. The old man caught hold of a limb and pulled himself up.

"The horses!" he gasped.

Teddy sped across to the shed. He untied the terrified mare, forced her, rearing and whinnying, across the clearing. Timothy grabbed the saddle horn. With the boy shoving, lifting, he struggled into the saddle.

The fire was coming with a roar. Flames crackled through the trees. A weird yellow glow lit up the clearing.

Teddy raced over to Concho, untied him, flung himself into the saddle. Sparks showered the clearing. Great waves of blinding smoke rolled through the trees.

"Quick!" the boy screamed.

With the wildly barking hound pup streaking out in front, the old man and the boy sent their horses at a run down the trail out of the clearing.

16

Thunder River Canyon drowsed in the warmth of the morning sun. The river sang around gray boulders, churning, swirling, on its way down canyon. In the glider on the porch deck, Timothy shifted stiffly against the pillows. One hand felt gingerly of the bandage binding his forehead.

Patricia glanced up from the book she was reading. "Want to change positions?" she asked. "Teddy, help Timothy."

Teddy scrambled up from where he and the hound pup lay sprawled on the floor. He went over to the glider, put his hands under Timothy's arms, eased him up higher on the pillows.

"Confounded young doctor, strapping me up so I can't breathe," Timothy grumbled, straightening the black patch over his eye.

Teddy grinned. "You want to get those ribs healed, don't you?" he asked.

Timothy reached up, rumbled the boy's brown hair. "And a fine-looking fellow you are," he said gruffly. "Eyebrows singed off. A scab as big as a dime on the end of your nose."

Teddy felt tenderly of his nose. "Scab's ready to come loose," he said cheerfully, "and Aunt Pat says my eyebrows'll grow out good as new. The burn on Mark's back is healed already. Come here, Mark. See, Timothy, his scab's come off."

"The pup'll likely grow a patch of white hair where he was burned," the old man grumbled.

Teddy knelt down and hugged the pup to him. "Mark'll still be beautiful," he said stoutly.

Patricia looked up at the mountains. "I'll be glad when the smoke clears up," she said slowly. "Every time I see it hanging there over Lobo and Arrowhead, I get sick all over again."

"Ten thousand acres of prime timber burned," Timothy said grimly. "Teddy here will live to see it come back, Pat, but you and I won't."

"But it could have been twenty thousand just as easily," she said sensibly, "if the rain hadn't come when it did and put the fire out." She glanced down at her hands, held them up. "Timothy, look. When will my hands stop shaking every time I think of that awful day?"

"They'll stop, Pat," the old man said slowly. "Things fade after a bit, even bad things. But you and I and Teddy here, we won't ever forget that fire. We've cause not to."

"When I remember how Forest Service told me on the phone their helicopter had crashed,"—she shuddered —"and then when I got back up to your place and found Teddy gone—" she broke off. "Heavens, that station wagon's turning in here. More tourists asking if the canyon's safe from fire!"

Teddy raised up on his knees. "That's a Buick, 1963," he announced. "Look, New York license plates."

"You go see what they want, Teddy," his aunt begged. "I don't feel up to telling one more tourist about our fire."

"Sure, I'll go." Teddy scrambled to his feet. "Come on, Mark. Golly, they just barely made the bridge. There's a boy getting—why, it's Clarence! It's Clarence!"

He was gone with a shout down the steps, the hound pup at his heels. Behind him Patricia gave Timothy one stricken look and started slowly toward the steps.

Beside the station wagon Teddy and a short, fat, tow-headed boy were pummeling each other with enthusiastic shouts, the hound pup leaping around them, barking wildly. A gray French poodle added shrill yips from the station wagon. The plump man and woman in the front seat beamed as Patricia approached. The man opened the door and got out.

"You're Pat," he said, shaking hands. "I'm Ed Burke, and this is Helen."

Patricia reached into the car, shook hands with Helen Burke. "Get out and come in," she said over the din of boys and dogs.

Teddy dragged the fat towhead around to his aunt. "This is Clarence, Aunt Pat," he beamed.

Patricia shook a limp, pudgy hand. "Hello, Clarence," she smiled. "I've heard a lot about you."

"Yes'm," he murmured, looking past her at the cabin. "Cool, I'll say! But where's your antenna? You on a cable out here?"

"No antenna," Teddy told him cheerfully, "and we're not on a cable. Come on, I want you to meet Timothy."

Somehow they all managed to get up the steps. Patricia introduced the Burkes to Timothy, helped Ed Burke drag chairs over close to the glider. The boys had fallen suddenly silent, eyeing each other with shyness born of months of separation.

"Nice place you've got here," Ed Burke beamed at Patricia.

"Thank you. We like it."

"Well, it's romantic," Helen Burke murmured, glancing up at the mountains. "Goodness, that smoke," she shuddered. "That must be where that horrible forest fire was. The radio and the papers were full of it. Weren't you thankful you were this far away from it! Is it safe here now?"

Patricia glanced from Timothy to Teddy. The old man kept silent. "The fire's been out five days, Aunt Helen," Teddy said, and nothing more.

She turned to him. "Teddy, come here and let Aunt Helen look at you. Heavens, you're skinny as a rail!"

"I bet you were surprised to see us, Fatso," Clarence broke in with a grin. "Mama and Papa wanted to wire we were coming, but I made them surprise you."

"We got into Denver last night," Helen Burke told Patricia. "Clarence wanted us to drive out here, then and there. Imagine, at night! Ed got us lost three times to-day and in broad daylight. I was awfully afraid you might already have moved into town for the winter. Thunder River Canyon was the only address we had."

"I don't move," Patricia said calmly. "This is my home. I live here the year around."

"But you do teach school?" Helen Burke said uncertainly.

"There's a swell Trading Post just ten miles on up the highway, Aunt Helen," Teddy broke in eagerly. "That's where Aunt Pat's school is. And the hospital, too, where Timothy's been. We just brought him home last night."

"A Trading Post," Helen Burke echoed. "Not even a town?"

The eagerness faded from the boy's eyes. He stood looking at her.

Ed Burke broke the awkward silence. "Been sick, eh?" he asked Timothy.

The old man shook his head. "Just a couple of cracked ribs," he said matter-of-factly. "Fool thing to stick a fellow in a hospital for a couple of cracked ribs, but I guess the medics have to get their hands on somebody to practice on."

"What happened to your eyebrows, Fatso?" Clarence asked Teddy. "Who skinned your nose?"

"Got too close to a match while I was lighting the stove," said Teddy, grinning.

"Same old clumsy Fatso," Clarence chuckled. Then he sobered, looking at Teddy uncertainly. "You know, Fatso just don't sound right any more," he grumbled. "I bet the fellows at school will change your name to String Bean this year."

Teddy's grin faded. He said nothing.

"I didn't catch your name when Pat introduced us," Ed Burke said to Timothy. "You a relative?"

"Trich," Timothy told him. "T-r-i-c-h. I'm just a neighbor. Pat and Teddy took me in because I was bunged up."

"Trich," Ed Burke repeated slowly. "That's not a common name. There's a fellow always being written up in hunting magazines—" he broke off, staring. "Timothy Trich. Say, you're not—"

"Timothy's just about the most famous hunter in the whole country," Teddy said proudly.

"Well, I never thought I'd ever meet Timothy Trich," Ed Burke said respectfully. "Wait till the boys at my club hear about this."

At that moment there came a shrill, demanding barking from the station wagon.

"Fifi!" Helen Burke cried. "Fifi wants out." She turned, eyed Mark. "Teddy, would you mind taking that—that hound dog away somewhere? I wouldn't want Fifi getting fleas."

Teddy's face flushed. He caught hold of Mark's collar, turned with him toward the cabin door. At the door he stopped, looked back, head high. "Mark doesn't have fleas, Aunt Helen," he said in a flat, tight voice. "I'll take Mark inside, so you can let Fifi out, but please, you mustn't call Mark a hound dog, like that. Mark's a pedigreed hound. Marcus Antonius, out of Queen Esther, by Julius Caesar. It's on his collar here."

Helen Burke bridled. "Well!"

"Timothy bred Mark," the boy went on in the same tight, flat voice. "Timothy doesn't have anything except purebreds. The males in Mark's litter all sold for five hundred dollars apiece." He opened the screened door and led Mark inside.

Ed Burke snorted gleefully. "Guess you got your comeuppance that time, Helen," he chuckled. "You didn't pay but a hundred fifty for that pedicured poodle of yours."

"I didn't mean to hurt your feelings, Teddy," Helen Burke apologized as the boy came back out onto the deck alone. "It's just—you know yourself, Teddy, how nervous Fifi always gets around another dog."

"Oh, you didn't hurt my feelings, Aunt Helen," the boy told her. "It was Mark's feelings I was worried about. Mark's not used to being called a hound dog, like that. I'll go let Fifi out now." He turned toward the steps. "Come on, Clarence."

"If we let Fifi out, we'll be an hour catching her again," Clarence protested. "I want to go back to Denver, Mama. You promised we could go to the movies. Why can't Fatso pack his things and we get going?"

Helen Burke looked from her son to Patricia. "We haven't even talked with Teddy's aunt yet about taking

Teddy back with us," she said hesitantly. "Teddy did tell you," she asked Patricia, "that we want to send him through prep school along with Clarence?"

Patricia glanced helplessly toward Teddy. He had halted on the top step and was standing motionless, his back to them. "Teddy showed me Clarence's letter," Patricia said slowly.

"I know I should have written you," Helen Burke said apologetically, "but like I told Ed, I'd rather we talk the whole thing out, all of us together."

Patricia nodded.

"Clarence has been simply lost with Teddy gone," Helen Burke went on. "You know that Teddy's been almost like our own ever since your sister died. His father was our best friend—and of course, your sister and I were friends for years."

"I know," Patricia said in a low voice. "She wrote me about you often."

"We'll take good care of the boy, Pat," Ed Burke said heartily. "And if you want, we can ship him out to you for vacations."

Patricia looked at them. "I know that you would be good to Teddy," she said quietly, "and don't think for a moment I don't realize what an opportunity you're offering him. That's why I can't say no. I don't feel that I have the right to stand between Teddy and such an opportunity."

"Well, then, that's settled," Ed Burke said jovially.

"Wait!" Patricia's voice was sharp. "I haven't finished. I said I couldn't stand in Teddy's way, and I won't. But there's more to it than that. I love Teddy. I couldn't love him more if he were my own son. And

Timothy loves him just as much. I don't know how to say it exactly, but since Teddy's been here, we've grown to be a family, Teddy and Timothy and Mark and I."

She stopped, cleared her throat huskily. "Timothy and Mark and I want him, too," she went on after a moment. "We want him very much. It's an awful responsibility to put on an eleven-year-old boy, having to decide how to live his life, but the decision must be Teddy's, not mine."

"I guess we didn't stop to think about your feeling so strongly about this," Ed Burke said slowly. He looked across at Teddy. "Well, Teddy?"

Teddy turned around slowly. He looked at them with troubled eyes.

"When Clarence's letter first came, Uncle Ed," he said hesitantly, "I was awfully glad. I was so homesick for you and Aunt Helen and Clarence, I was just miserable. And I hated the mountains. I just couldn't wait to get back to New York."

He stopped, looked up at the mountains, frowned. "Then, lots of things happened," he went on after a moment. "Aunt Pat was so good to me, and she'd bought me a horse of my very own—" The boy's eyes lighted. "He's a buckskin—his name's Concho. And then Timothy started taking me out in the mountains with the dogs. Timothy taught me to fly-fish, and he taught me to shoot a rifle, and he taught me to see things I'd never seen before, and how to listen—"

He looked at them, brown eyes clear and honest. "I guess I started growing up," he said slowly, "only I didn't know it. I started liking to read. I've read every one of my Aunt Pat's books, and now she's started me on some more. And I've read all the magazine stories about Timothy. And I don't miss TV any more, or the movies."

He broke off, glanced at the hound pup sitting with head cocked just inside the screened door. "And then there's Mark," he said in a low voice.

"Mark?" Ed Burke echoed. "What's the hound got to do with it?"

"Mark's mine, Uncle Ed," the boy said eagerly. "Timothy gave him to me. Me and Timothy, we're partners. We're going to breed up the best line of hounds in the whole country."

"You mean you're not going back with us, Teddy?" Helen Burke asked incredulously.

"Aw, Fatso!" Clarence protested.

"I can't," Teddy stammered, "I just can't. I love you, Aunt Helen, and Uncle Ed and Clarence, but I love my Aunt Pat and Timothy, too. I just don't think I could stay away from them or from the mountains and Mark."

He ran across to the door, opened it. The hound pup came bounding out. Teddy knelt down, put both arms around the wriggling pup. "Me and Mark—we've been through a lot together," he said thickly. "I couldn't go off and leave Mark. Just like I couldn't go off and leave Timothy and Aunt Pat."

Patricia went to him. Teddy got to his feet. His aunt put her arms around him. She looked at the Burkes over his head. "I'm sorry," she said simply.

Ed Burke cleared his throat. "We sure don't want to force the boy to—I mean, we thought—" he broke off.

Timothy spoke up for the first time. "You meant it for the best, Ed," he said comfortingly. "You and your good wife, and your boy there. What Teddy said a minute ago about his changing, Ed—the lad's right. He has grown up. Seems like he's found himself, somehow. Got his feet planted firmly. Knows what he wants to do."

Timothy paused, looked up at the mountains, his blue eye shining. "The lad hears his drummer," he said softly. "Maybe distant, far away, but he hears the music he's marching to. Yes sir, the lad hears the music he's marching to."

About the Author

MARTHA MILLER is the pseudonym of Martha Ivan. She is married to Gus Ivan, with whom she has worked in collaboration on four books for boys and girls, under the pseudonym of Gus Tavo.

As a young girl on the West Texas plains, Mrs. Ivan spent her summers on cattle ranches, where she learned to ride and hunt. She and Mr. Ivan love the outdoors, and spend their summers in the West—New Mexico, Colorado (where TIMBERLINE HOUND is laid), South Dakota, Wyoming (scene of their last book, TRACK THE GRIZZLY DOWN), Southern California. In their travels they visit zoos and national parks, spending long hours watching and studying such wild animals as cougars, grizzly bears, or buffaloes, so that they can write convincing stories about the wildlife of the West.

Mrs. Ivan holds a B.A. and an M.A. in English from Texas Technological College, and did graduate work at the University of Texas and the University of California. Formerly chairman of the English department at Kilgore College, she is now Director of Guidance.

A Note on the Type

This book was set on the Linotype in Janson, a recutting made direct from the type cast from matrices made by Anton Janson. Whether or not Janson was of Dutch ancestry is not known, but it is known that he purchased a foundry and was a practicing type-founder in Leipzig during the years 1660 to 1687. Janson's first specimen sheet was issued in 1675. His successor issued a specimen sheet showing all of the Janson types in 1689.

His type is an excellent example of the influential and sturdy Dutch types that prevailed in England prior to the development by William Caslon of his own incomparable designs, which he evolved from these Dutch faces. The Dutch in their turn had been influenced by Garamond in France. The general tone of Janson, however, is darker than Garamond and has a sturdiness and substance quite different from its predecessors. It is a highly legible type, and its individual letters have a pleasing variety of design. Its heavy and light strokes make it sharp and clear, and the full-page effect is characterful and harmonious.